More Advance Praise for

"In *Festival Man*, [Geoff Berner] cuts a
scene with an antic and destructively hilarious scythe. This novel is so
subversively good, so profanely sacred, with its global savvy and deluded
genius anti-hero, that I'm torn between hiding it from my thirteen-year-
old son (a Berner fan) or propping it up against his cereal bowl."
— ZSUZSI GARTNER, AUTHOR OF THE GILLER PRIZE–NOMINATED
BETTER LIVING THROUGH PLASTIC EXPLOSIVES

"Spare and pointed, yet willfully ticklish, Geoff Berner's fictional debut
chimes with summer truths and rock and roll lies. A great companion to
any Canadian road trip going from here to there."
— DAVE BIDINI, AUTHOR OF *WRITING GORDON LIGHTFOOT: THE MAN, THE MUSIC, AND THE
WORLD IN 1972* AND *ON A COLD ROAD: TALES OF ADVENTURE IN CANADIAN ROCK*

"Filled with rock 'n' roll adventure and emotional debris, Campbell's speed-
and-booze-fuelled ramblings reflect — accurately and often hilariously —
the unconventional characters who exist within the music industry."
— *QUILL & QUIRE*

"A demented part of me hopes the suction cups hanging Mr. Geoff
Berner to the side of the planet will lose their grip and that he, and his
manuscript, will hurl off. Because then I can steal a bunch of his lines
— lines I would have written if only I'd thought of them myself."
— SUSAN MUSGRAVE, AUTHOR OF *KISS TICKLE CUDDLE HUG* AND
YOU'RE IN CANADA NOW, MOTHERFUCKER

"If I ever rise up out of prison, the first thing I am going to do is buy
Geoff Berner's book. Well, maybe the second thing …"
— STEPHEN REID, AUTHOR OF *JACKRABBIT PAROLE* AND *A CROWBAR IN THE BUDDHIST GARDEN*

"A blind sleigh ride through more of the music business — with a
side of Canadian-eh? good-natured desperation — than most decent
readers might be bargaining for. Warning, amid the fun and frolic
there is much to fear here!"
— DENNIS. E. BOLEN, AUTHOR OF *ANTICIPATE RESULTS* AND *KASPLOIT!*

Early drafts of the chapters "A Note on Festivals" and
"Manny at North Country Fair" first appeared as
excerpted pieces in *BC Musician Magazine*.

FESTIVAL MAN

GEOFF BERNER

DUNDURN
TORONTO

Editor: Shannon Whibbs
Design: Courtney Horner
Printer: Webcom

Library and Archives Canada Cataloguing in Publication

Berner, Geoff, 1971-
        Festival man / Geoff Berner.

Issued also in electronic formats.
ISBN 978-1-4597-0724-5

        I. Title.

PS8603.E7353F47 2013   C813'.6   C2012-908617-7

1   2   3   4   5   17   16   15   14   13

We acknowledge the support of the **Canada Council for the Arts** and the **Ontario Arts Council** for our publishing program. We also acknowledge the financial support of the **Government of Canada** through the **Canada Book Fund** and **Livres Canada Books**, and the **Government of Ontario** through the **Ontario Book Publishing Tax Credit** and the **Ontario Media Development Corporation**.

Care has been taken to trace the ownership of copyright material used in this book. The author and the publisher welcome any information enabling them to rectify any references or credits in subsequent editions.

J. Kirk Howard, President

The publisher is not responsible for websites or their content unless they are owned by the publisher.

Printed and bound in Canada.

Visit us at
Dundurn.com
@dundurnpress
Facebook.com/dundurnpress
Pinterest.com/dundurnpress

Dundurn	Gazelle Book Services Limited	Dundurn
3 Church Street, Suite 500	White Cross Mills	2250 Military Road
Toronto, Ontario, Canada	High Town, Lancaster, England	Tonawanda, NY
M5E 1M2	LA1 4XS	U.S.A. 14150

These are the Memoirs of Campbell Ouiniette, former head of Bombsmuggler Incorporated Music, manager at one time or another of many illustrious folk, country, punk, and world music artists.

The stack of copiously stained, longhand-scrawled legal notepads were found in October 2003, outside Pincher Creek, Alberta, by accordionist and archivist Geoff Berner, who also managed to decipher Ouiniette's idiosyncratic handwriting.

FESTIVAL MAN

"Without cruelty, there is no festival."
— Friedrich Nietzsche, *On the Genealogy of Morality*

I BOUGHT THIS FARMHOUSE FOR A DOLLAR. Which I actually haven't paid yet. I shouldn't be here. I should be headed home. But I can't go home empty-handed, so I have decided to sit down in this empty, run-down-but-still-standing discarded house, and write a proper account of how the whole thing went down last weekend, in Calgary. I feel the need to make an accounting of myself.

Why? Because I know that a lot of people think of me as worthless. Less than worthless; a parasite, dragging other people down, a rip-off artist.

I know their nicknames for me, "Scam-Bull." "Mr. 'No Problem.'" I was given an Indian name once, a good one, which spoke of my bravery and rare insight. That name was later redacted by the name-giver to "Skid Mark." They say I'm incompetent, a liar, an Alcoholic. One musician who I still think of as a friend will tell anybody who asks about me that I'm the kind of guy who'd sell his own grandmother and still not manage to make a profit. How do you like that? And in a certain light, maybe they're right. But for the sake of Posterity, for the sake of my Love, at home in Vancouver, my Love whose regard for me I know has been ebbing away like a slow leak in an old truck tire, and for my daughter, too, maybe when she's old enough, after she's heard all the innuendo and bullshit talked about me, there needs to be a document that shows *my light* on things.

I've always sworn I'd never write my *memoirs*. I've always thought of the written word, unaccompanied by music, as a guaranteed lie, deliberate or otherwise. So this will not be that. It's just an account sheet summary of this past weekend, skipping over irrelevant details, focusing on the key points, and, most importantly, explaining from my point of view what was *really* going on, under the surface of the events themselves, especially my intentions, my goals, the reasoning *behind* my actions, actions which I know, on the face of things, might look a bit questionable to some people.

The key is to keep that focus, to stick to the story, and not get distracted into digression. Above all, I have to *make sure* to stay solidly on track, telling the events of this past weekend. It should run no more than four or five pages, which is good because my arm is pretty badly chewed up and I'm afraid it may be starting to worsen a bit. Right arm, though, so I can still write through the pain, as I'm left-handed.

So I'm holed up here in this house that I bought for a dollar. I just own the house, not the land around the house. You can do that around here, just by finding a number on a truckstop bulletin board and meeting a guy at a diner in town. That's "'cause this is where the big agribusinesses have bought out all the family farms to create food factories the size of Belgium. It's not cost-efficient to bulldoze all the little grey houses that dot the Canadian prairies. You might as well just leave them standing there, an accidental warning, like the statues on Easter Island. They're not hooked up to the electricity grid or water anymore, but it's summer, and there's some buckets around, and a river not too far away that I can get to in the rental minivan that I should have returned four days ago.

I stopped at the store on the way here, so I've got a bunch of good Alberta Beef jerky, a bag of tomatoes, a roll of bandage tape, and a bottle of whiskey, not for the purpose of getting drunk, mostly just for sterilizing the wounds in the arm, but also to use to wean myself off the booze a bit, which may be overdue, I guess. Don't want to get the d.t.'s — you can die of that. I've seen it. And of course, I've got a bunch of speed, in powdered, snortable form, to keep the words coming efficiently. I have candles, too, so I can work through the night.

THE COLLECTOR

LET ME TELL YOU WHAT I AM.

I'm quite a big man, if I do say so myself, about six foot two, and broad-shouldered, with a measure of heft. Not fat, but some heft. I've got a mighty puff of unruly, dirty-blond curly hair that kind of emanates from my head and face and makes me look even bigger. I think it's fair to say that, for better or for worse, I take up a lot of space. Not just physically; I project. I don't care much about clothes. I tend to wear the same green sweatpants and black hoodie everywhere I go, whether I'm in the alley behind some dank rock club, or at some idiotic music industry awards gala. I smell like drum tobacco and dope and thick cowboy coffee and eastern European delicatessen meat. And sweat, probably.

I look big, but I rarely get into actual fistfights, and although I can't say I've ever won a brawl in a bar, I'm usually able to stick to the Golden Rule of Canadian Bar Fighting and inflict roughly as much damage on my assailant as he has done unto me.

I'm not a musician. I make music happen. Yes, I've played music, but only when it was the last option, in order to make the music happen. I played the bass a few times because no one else wanted to play the bass, and otherwise that band would not have happened, so I did what had to be done. I wasn't bad. That's the good thing about electric bass — it's very hard to be noticed as a great bass player — people only notice the bass as the general sound of the band — but the corollary is that it's hard to be noticed as bad. Not like what I do now. Everyone knows I'm bad. I'm a bad man, a bad drunk, a tornado of chaos, harbinger of strange music. Only some of them appreciate how important that makes me in this world.

I STARTED OUT COLLECTING RECORDS, growing up on a horse ranch outside a mid-sized town in Alberta. First I just bought albums from Kelly's Music World at the strip mall. Then I noticed some of the albums had catalogues in them, so I sent away for more albums. Then I started bugging my mother to drive me into Edmonton to finger through the vinyl at the record stores near the university. I started talking to the music twerps who worked there, and that's when I got truly, absolutely hooked, saving up my chore money for the rare stuff, getting in touch with other weirdos. Still remember tearing the brown paper off the bootleg copy of the Rolling Stones' *Cocksucker Blues*, thinking, this is contraband from another, more exciting universe. This is *nasty*. This is worth staying alive for.

It was a completely seamless step for me, from collecting rare music to collecting rare musicians. I met Sandy Mackenzie when we were both seventeen, in a record store that isn't there anymore, on Whyte Avenue in Edmonton. We both reached for the same 45, "Hamburger Lady," by Throbbing Gristle ("Burned from the waist up, she's dying") and immediately got to talking. I told him that I'd tape the single and let him have the tape for free if he'd let me buy the only copy in the store. He said he just wanted to hear it a couple of times, 'cause he wanted *his band* to cover it.

Sandy was the first person I ever met who was actually in a band. Okay, there were the horrifying sad country bands that did the shitheel circuit of rural Alberta, playing Charlie Pride and Conway Twitty covers, but that didn't count. I was intrigued. I kidnapped him and dragged him back to the empty house some friends and I had been squatting. We listened to "Hamburger

Lady" over and over again, and he told me about how he wasn't sure, but he thought his band might be pretty fucking good. Maybe even as good as the Modern Minds, some nerdy XTC fans from Saskatchewan that he idolized.

Sandy was wrong about his band. They were fucking *fantastic*. They didn't even know how good they were. That was my job.

I was ecstatically, devoutly *in love* with the sound that band made. I would just sit crouched in the corner of their foul, dusty practice space in Sandy's mom's basement, drinking hi-test beer and rocking back and forth like an autistic monk. The dryer didn't vent properly and I still remember the warm, wet denim smell of that place, mixed with the malt of new and old beer.

The sound hadn't been quantified and qualified and marketified yet. The people playing it didn't know it was hardcore punk rock. Machine-gun drums, random, power-saw guitar, urgent, thudding, repetitive bass, and screaming lyrics full of everything you *wished you'd said* when you were being chewed out by the principal, the cop, the manager of the 7-Eleven. Of course it sounded like "a bunch of noise" — it was the sound of breaking out of being trapped. That's what real freedom sounds like, motherfucker, not that *you* would recognize it.

I'll never know where I got this instinct, but I found myself desperately wanting to share that sound with the world, to see what it would do to people. I was sure that if they could hear it, some of them, just some of them, mind you, would *change* before my eyes, just as the music was changing me. One day, I stood up from my corner in the practice space, and told them that they had one month to be ready, because I was going to get them their first show. They gave me a look I'm now used to, that mixture of awe and suspicion, the excitement of *wanting* to believe, combined with the stubborn Albertan certainty they'd been raised with: that interesting things only happened to other people, people on TV or something. But even if they were pretty sure I wouldn't be able to do it, they still desperately *wanted* me to be able to do it. They couldn't hide that. With that look, they invested me with their hopes, despite themselves in spite of themselves.

Naturally, I hadn't a clue how I was going to do it, besides some vague notions I'd derived from "the early years" segments of rock-star biographies, but the certainty with which I said it was enough to magnetize the band to my nonexistent plan.

That first show I put on, thank God I was an indigent at the time. The money we lost on renting the hall, the posters, the P.A. rental — I could walk away from it, because I owned no assets to seize and had no place to live. Deep down, I guess I knew that I had no idea what I was doing, because at least I'd made the wise decision to put my last Social Studies teacher's address on the forms the hall custodian put in front of me. That was the last time I have ever had the poor judgment to promote a concert under my own legal name. Maybe the key lesson of that first show was that you can't put on a financially successful concert by marketing only to people who are just like you. Especially if you yourself are penniless, and you enjoy breaking things. Whatever the lesson was, I've met about three thousand people who claim to have been among that sad little dimly lit smattering of ugly kids in torn denim. The crowd was so sparse that when they attempted to slam dance, about half the time they missed slamming into anybody, instead tumbling and sliding in the broken glass and beer that they'd stamped into the old hardwood floor.

Had to leave town for a few months after that one. Went and worked on the neighbour's ranch back in the sticks. Even saw my old man a couple times, stalking the perimeter of our property with a mickey of Golden Wedding on his tool belt.

When I came back, the band had transformed. Without a place to play in public, or an audience, or jobs, or any money, or girlfriends, or anything to do, the group had festered delightfully in the basement till it was powerful, corrosive, unstoppable — like black mould. The playing and the songs were so much stronger, tougher, more pointedly aggressive. Meanwhile, in the outside world, a goodly chunk of the kids had finally got tired of New Romantic schlock and smarmy white disco. The boil was engorged. I just had to pop it.

I went around to the bars, demanding that they book us. I told them that if they didn't agree to hire us now, they'd be begging us to play there in six months, and by then we'd be demanding ten times the money. Each time I finished making that pitch, I paused, waiting for the bar owner to respond, certain that he'd be swept up in my atomic tsunami of enthusiasm. I was very young.

So it was back to renting halls for us. This time, I picked the Polish Community Hall, across the river in the nicer part of town, instead of the scummy former church I'd rented downtown the last time. It was more expensive, but I reasoned that more parents would let their kids go there. I talked Sandy's mother into giving us the cash for the deposit. She was feeling guilty about the divorce, so frankly, I barely had to manipulate her at all.

Then we just promoted the living Hell out of it. We postered over every other poster on the street with past-due canned condensed milk for glue. Takes hours to get that shit off. You need a chisel and a bucket of industrial solvent. We hung around the high schools, giving out handbills with the gig details and big bold print that said "Fuck Your ..." and then a long list of things that ought to be fucked. Kids love that.

Even after we had paid the whole (woefully inadequate, it would turn out) damage deposit, the gig was a financial success, by our standards. And it was a perfect evening.

Fuck! The sense of release, the exhilaration in the boys' and girls' whole bodies, as they hurled themselves around the hall, bashing into each other, bashing into the stage, bashing into the band. These kids who had been waiting all their lives for this band, this music, these songs to come along. Finally, somebody with access to a VERY LOUD sound system was saying everything they'd been dying to say to the people who'd been crushing their horizons and sense of self-worth since they could crawl.

"What's wrong with you? Are you stupid? Who do you think you are? You think the world owes you a living?"

"Oh yeah? FUCK YOU! I'm a punk rocker now! Look at me! I'm a disgrace to everything you believe in! Go tell the priest, the school, your boss, that you all failed as authority figures, that my very identity is an incontrovertible rebuke to your values — I'm living proof that you're a wash-out as a parent, because I'm a *punk rocker!"*

And once a bunch of kids decide that an event is the place to go on a Saturday night, a bunch of other kids come, too.

These were the kids who had no idea this kind of thing even existed. Children of comfort, of affluence, whose parents voted Conservative, not out of the usual idiot false consciousness, but because it aligned directly with their interests as members of the elite one-party Petrolaucracy of Oilberta.

You could see the fear in their eyes, as they watched the Rabble celebrate their Rabbleness. It was Magic. We were comforting, no, *thrilling*, the afflicted, and giving the complacent a good, honest scare.

Also, we all got laid.

After a few shows we had the money thing down to a science. Sandy and I would sit with a bottle of Bulgarian wine and his little cigarette maker and spend an afternoon calculating out the best way to relieve a middle class kid of his entire week's allowance.

> Admission: $4
> 5-Song home-duplicated cassette of band in
> practice space: $4
> Band shirt (band logo spray-painted on random
> 50-cent Salvation Army rag): $6
> Band pin: a buck.
> Sticker: 'nother buck.
> Poster: $2

And I made a good side business out of selling pre-rolled joints and speedy acid. Okay, well, that was more like where most of the real profit came from. And so it ever shall be.

We had a good run for about nine months. I started hearing from other bands that would get in touch, looking for a gig. I was getting known as a guy who got shit going. When things became muddled or confusing, the band, and others, too, would look to me, because they knew I would always come up with a strong opinion. Later, they could bitch about me talking bullshit, and say that I was steamrolling them into disaster, but they still counted on me as the only person in the room who could forcefully state that he Knew What to Do. People started to call me the band's "manager."

Then Sandy's sister committed suicide, and we all took a break for a while.

MY PLAN

BUT THAT WAS A LONG TIME AGO, and it was just by way of telling you what a genuinely extraordinary sort of fellow I am — my important strengths in terms of my ability to inspire, my vision, my perfect sense of art, my knack for Making Things Happen, et cetera. I return now to the story of what happened at the Calgary Folk Festival last weekend, which is what this is all about, of course.

I WAS ON MY WAY TO THE CALGARY Folk Festival, without the headliner. I was beer-drunk, and more or less out of money, but I had a plan.

The previous winter, I had discovered Athena Amarok, and managed to book her for every major summer folk music festival in the country, on the strength of a grainy Betacam tape of her performance at the Opening Ceremonies of the Canada Northern Games, in Iqualuit, and of course also on the strength of my nigh-irresistible persuasive powers.

I knew she was going to be a killer success. She was young, sexy, and had a sound that no one had ever heard before. Plus she was Inuit, and the Leftiness of the Canadian folk circuit is always dying to book "First Nations" people, so that they (the folkies) can demonstrate their Super-Virtue and Lack of Prejudice and what-have-you. And here was a Genuine Eskimo who made everybody who heard her simultaneously terrified and sexually aroused. I knew I was on to a winner.

The only problem was, she was even more of a winner than I'd planned for. After the first performance I arranged for her in the South (as the Yukoners call it, "South" meaning the Whole Wicked Rest of the World Below the Arctic Circle) some journalist jerk from Iceland had seen her and sent a tape of the show straight to this crazy Icelandic experimental disco Superstar, and this had caused the Superstar, when she saw it, to "change her whole thinking about music forever," and so of course she emailed Athena directly to invite her to New York on the first available plane, to "see if we could collaborate," and then naturally that led her to fall in love with Athena and invite her on tour immediately, and although I made some perfunctory attempt at stopping her, you can't say no to Superstars, so in fact, at this moment, as we drove towards Calgary, Athena was actually in Reykjavik, where she was participating in the secret rehearsals for the Giant World Tour, slated to start in a week and a half in London.

So Athena was in fact *not* going to be at the Calgary Folk Festival, nor was she going to be at three of the five other festivals that I had already negotiated large guaranteed fees for, fees that, just by the way, I had already spent the entirety of, in the form of advances from said guarantees. Yes, I know. But that money *had* to be spent. Which is something I will explain. But right now, I'm explaining my plan.

So here was my plan:

First of all, nobody *knew* that Athena wasn't coming. Using the management tool called Guilt, I had extracted her secrecy about her Big Break, since I personally, after all, was the one responsible for it happening. Also, even more importantly, nobody knew that *I knew* that Athena wasn't coming, and had known for about four weeks. Four weeks would have been long enough in advance for the artistic director of the festival to cancel her contract and scramble to make other plans for a Sunday headliner set. But we couldn't have that. That wasn't part of the plan. So that's the first of all.

Second, and more importantly, I still had her band with me.

The plan all along, once I figured out what I had in Athena, was to use her as a kind of Arctic Trojan Horse, to help me sneak some of my most interesting (weirdest) acts inside the Hallowed Gates of the Folk Festivals. Festivals are generally very conservative, and tend to book things that are easily explainable. African Drumming. Traditional Celtic Harp. Third-Rate Ontario Bluegrass. I generally go for stuff that's very hard to explain, but is the kind of thing that if you see it live and you're not some boring asshole, it amazes you about the possibilities of music, and the permutations of the human mind and soul. But those hard-to-explain things can often be kind of hard to sell to the bookers. So the plan all along was to get my weird people through the gates, disguised as Athena's band.

As band leader I had Jenny Reid, a lesbian singer-songwriter-bass-drums-and-saxophone player who sings songs so sexually aggressive that if a man sang them, he'd be tarred and feathered as a misogynist pig. Then there was a turntablist, guitar player, weird sound-maker and interpretive-dancer named Manny Canoe, and, as a last-minute addition, there was Mykola Loychuck, a 220-pound kobza-playing singer-songwriter of Ukrainian descent, who plays a combination of traditional Ukrainian songs, translated into English in an offensive way, and original Ukrainian-sounding songs that are also mostly offensive. That was the band. It was supposed to have had that lying Jew bastard accordion player Berner, but he had taken off without warning for some wild-goose chase in the backwoods of Bulgaria, hunting for nonagenarian kyke fiddlers or some such nonsense. Good riddance if he wanted to miss this opportunity after all I did for him.

Anyway, the band had been working. The weirdness of the group underlined the weirdness of Athena, who was by no means a conventional Inuit throat-singer. She'd been denounced in the local papers as a cultural heretic and sexual deviant. People in Iqualuit threw rocks at her when they saw her on the street, so she was very much one of My Kind of People. And the fact that the band were actually all experienced improvisers, and surprisingly good at listening to each other and to Athena, meant that each performance was an unrepeatably odd, but oddly musical event. People didn't just dance, they smashed things and fucked on the dancefloor. That's when you know that you're doing something right.

And from a manager's point of view, it was perfect, because these festivals are full of little stages, workshops, small performances, open mics, campfires, all places where you could actually put these strange people in front of an audience, so that they could finally just *be heard* by somebody. I'd just say to the artistic director of the festival, "Well, Mykola's here as Athena's kobza player, but he has a bunch of great tunes of his own. Maybe he should just sit in on the 'New Visions in Old Traditions' workshop." And then this unknown freak would be suddenly playing to a crowd of a thousand relaxed, *listening* people. And suddenly, the poor idiot savant bastard had some *fans*, for the first time in his life, for Chrissakes.

But that was when Athena had actually been *with* us for the festivals. Now I was going to try to blague my people through an entire large-scale, prestigious festival, sneaking them into the workshop stages, et cetera, when the actual marquee name of their band was not even going to be there.

My plan was to just keep acting expectant about her imminent arrival, showing myself to be getting more and more irritated, and then, maybe sometime on Saturday, totally blow my top, outraged, pretending to have just gotten a message from Athena saying that she had run off with the popstar. By this time, hopefully, her bandmates would be so successful that everyone would forgive the small problem of the lack of headliner, and the artistic director would have no choice but to let my weirdos play Athena's Sunday night huge-exposure main stage slot on their own, to shocked acclaim.

So THE MAIN PLAN WAS A BIT of a gamble, I know. I admit that. Then there was the long shot gamble:

Richard Wren was coming. Wren was the manager of Jimmy Kinnock, the world's most famous punk-folk singer, and was also the head of the International Conference of Music Managers. He had managed Cream when Clapton was good, was one of the organizers of the Rolling Stones' famous free concert in Hyde Park in memory of Brian Jones, where ten thousand doves were released into the audience, and had managed a little band called "The Clash" during the period when they had their only hits in America.

My plan with Wren was to find him, seduce him with my outsized and charming personality, get him drunk as a lord, and then bamboozle him into signing binding documents of commitment to co-manage and promote one or more of my artists (I hadn't decided exactly which yet), in partnership with Yours Truly, of course. I was carrying the legal papers on my person, blank in strategic spaces, easily alterable to suit my purposes, as the finer details of my purposes developed. I like to leave myself room to manoeuvre.

I knew that if I could pull all that off, I would be justified in continuing to speak of myself as a Genius. And I also knew, my Love, that I had to do something Genius to replenish the glamour that first drew you to me, long ago, when we first met. I knew that glamour had been receding for some time, as each successive heroic failure looked less heroic, and the low hum of collection-agency phone calls rose in frequency. I had made a conscious decision not to wonder if there was any point in returning home if I returned empty-handed.

How did I find Athena? That's what they all asked me, and that's why those festival directors still take my phone calls. Well, I don't know if they *still* take my phone calls, but they were taking them at the beginning of this summer, anyway. The truth of the matter, I can't emphasize enough for you young aspiring Campbells-to-be, is that to find the truly strange music, there's no easy shortcut around doing strange things, in strange places, with other strange people.

The previous winter, I had found myself, through a mixture of happenstance and self-interested chicanery, in a remote region of Canada's newest official territory, Nunavut, the place of the Inuit. I was in the capital, Iqaluit, for a conference of Northern bureaucrats, a conference for which I had obtained false credentials, in the interest of getting a chance to make contact with these two eighty-year-old ladies who did Inuit throat-singing, which is this breathy, growly music that they played up there as a kind of game between two girls to try to see who would crack up laughing first. Apparently it's funny to them, but the sound of it is evocative of a storm whipping furiously over an awe-inspiring, unspeakably vast Arctic landscape.

All attempts at finding electronic or postal means of communication with these ladies had been fruitless. I began to think that they were deliberately avoiding contact with southerners and their technology. But I had to have them. I'd heard them in a sample by this Mongolian electronica DJ, and I knew that if I could get even just a Dictaphone recording of their thing and whip up a one-page bio, I could probably book a full Canadian folk festival tour for them, with flights and all, and me getting 15 percent of the fee as booking agent, another 10 percent as manager, and then 15 percent of the Canada Council for the

Arts grants that I would "help" them apply for and that they'd inevitably get.*

So I had figured on catching these ladies' set, while scoping the room to see what younger relative was chaperoning them, translating for them, handling them. I would find that person and try to suss out by watching them what my way into their confidence ought to be. Would it be a young militant firebrand, who I could impress with outrageous political rhetoric and my connections to friends who were hereditary Blackfoot chiefs down in southern Alberta? Or would they be bloody Catholic goody-goodies (you'd be surprised how good I can be with Christians) who would respond to the idea of a tour as a kind of missionary appeal work? Or would I just do my usual and be the only guy in the place holding decent weed and hard liquor, get them matching me hoot for hoot, drink for drink, wait for them to get to the crucial vulnerable state, and then infuse my victims with my vision of descending on the southern folkies with the kind of music that would fill audiences with despair for the paucities of Western European culture?

I was standing in the gym at the opening ceremonies, sipping an energy drink and scanning the crowd for sexy octogenarians. The cheap institutional public address system whistled with feedback as the announcer spoke softly into the mic with an Inuit accent.

"We have a special treat today, ladies and gentleman. A young lady, who recently joined St. Margaret's Elementary school as a new teacher, a proud Inuit young lady who will demonstrate her skills at our own Inuit art of throat-singing. The young lady says that this is something she's been practising in her living room, by throat-singing alone with her record collection over the last three winters. I haven't heard it yet, but I'm sure it's going to be just dandy. Please welcome Athena Amarok."

---

* *If you think I'm the only one out there doing things that way, then you are a certifiable moron. Don't get me started.*

A small woman of about twenty-four walked shyly onto the stage. She was wearing a traditional cloak. She thanked the emcee and took the mic.

"Okay, well, I'm going to do my thing here, and I hope people don't think it's too strange. As you know, throat-singing is usually done with two people, I know, but I was a bit depressed sometimes in the winter, alone in my house, and I just sort of started doing this. You might not like it. Anyways ..."

Quietly at first, she started her back-and-forth, back-and-forth slow, flowing breathing, *humminah, humminah, humminah,* slowly adding a hint of something, a roughness that became a growl. The growl extended, mutated, grew, there was a sense of imminent threat in it now, the rhythm of the breathing carrying it with more urgency, and then suddenly it stopped.

And then the world exploded.

I guess I hadn't noticed the hip-hop kid hook up the decks to the PA, so when he dropped the beat at full force, it was like getting defibrillated. The room lit up for me. The scariest, bass-heaviest slouching-towards-Bethlehem backing track shook the architecture of the gymnasium, as Athena let forth a terrible howl like a giant wounded animal destroying an abattoir with its hind legs. Then the performance turned into this hypnotic, non-verbal explanation of the life of a woman from birth to death, and everything (*everything*) in the middle. It took about twenty minutes. When she stopped, everyone in the audience looked dazed, like they'd just awoken from a dream.

Once they woke up, a lot of them came to themselves and realized that they ought to be offended by such a brazen display. But not me. I had been waiting quite some time for an experience like that, and I knew exactly what to do. And I did it. And yes, then eventually I lost her, just like I lost many others. The important thing to note is that I lost her, not to the Big Time, but to the fact that I didn't have the Big Time clout that I rightfully ought to have had. So this Calgary Folk Festival was going to be different. This time I was going to light the rocket and remember to take care to hold on to it when it took off. And then people would finally understand me as the Visionary that I've always been. And Marina, you would go back to seeing me as the man of passion and courage who whisked you brilliantly out of Yugoslavia as it crumbled to ruin, not as the guy who rolls endless hash-and-drum smokes and talks endlessly at the kitchen table while the sad, desperate musicians troop in and out of our little Vancouver east-side apartment, hoping I can find them a break.

A REFLECTION ON FESTIVALS

I'VE HAD UNTOLD ADVENTURES at festivals, and without them I wouldn't have a career at all, I guess. Okay, well, possibly I now don't have a career, but you know what I mean.

A decent festival is always crazy, stupid, and beautiful.

Here's how you make a festival:

You gather thousands of people together in a place that's usually not considered fit for human habitation, like a farmer's field, or a racetrack, and then those people proceed to lay waste to the land and themselves for about two-to-three days or more. By the end, the people are exhausted, ravaged by the forces of nature and the forces of booze and drugs, and the land is a churned-up wound full of garbage, piss, and shit. People die, people are conceived, marriages begin or collapse. And there's music!

Somehow, magic emerges from the process. And everybody knows that the source of the magic is the music. I know that's a cliché, but nevertheless, it's just a fact, a fact that's as factual as E=MC squared or what-have-you. I can't state it plainer than that. Some people talk about "community" or whatever, but that's just a political word. Nothing against politics — politics can be a great source for wonderfully powerful songs. But when the music works, that's what makes the real sense of community happen. Everybody feeling the same thing at the same time, invisible tendrils of emotion stringing out from somewhere in the core of the musician, creeping into, yes, the souls of the people in the audience, fucking with their insides, messing with their way of being in the world. Changing them. I'm not into the stuff that soothes the savage breast. I want to see those savage breasts get all hot and bothered and get savage-er. That's my agenda.

That's why I'm so careful about working with the right musicians. Of course, almost all musicians wanna be rich and famous and get laid with people they have no right to be laid with. That's a given. But I can instantly spot the ones for whom that's the *only* reason they're into the music. The careerists. The ones who are solely concerned with "making it," whatever "it" is. I only work with people who expand my ideas about what people can think or feel, kind of illuminating their little corner of existence, without shame or hesitancy. That's the key to what makes me truly great.

And the musicians need to be able to embrace the festival-ness of festivals, the possibility that someone's, anyone's, life could be thrown sideways, just by the fact of being there, even accidentally, for just a verse of one song.

I remember seeing that brilliant old hustler, Leonard Cohen, at the Glastonbury Festival, the biggest festival in England. The drunk Jew Buddhist monk had spent so much time on some mountain, avoiding thoughts of worldly materialism, that the World, in the form of his minx of a manager, had stolen all his lucrative publishing rights away from him, and he had to hit the road to make a buck. I don't think he gave a shit where they put him, as long as he could make up for the five million the bitch had run off with. He'd made the mistake of fucking her, of course, so it served him right. Never play with your food, kids.

At first, it seemed like a shamefully bad idea to put the Poet Rabbi in front of 150,000 drunk, druggy, muddy English people. You could have got a similar auditory experience by sitting at home, putting on a Leonard Cohen record, then phoning up a bunch of rowdy football hooligans and inviting them over for a keg of lager. "I've seen the future, brother, it is murder," intoned the low, raspy voice, and his young, stupid audience seemed to be there for some kind of jaunty illustration of the lyric.

Then an odd thing happened. The band slowly summoned up (Cohen's band never could be described as "kicking in" to a song) the opening of "Hallelujah." I'd forgotten that mainstream English people love Jeff Buckley, for some reason, and that Buckley's one good recording was a cover of that. Immediately, the chavs started to hoot and scream, as if "Wonderwall" were coming on the stereo. And they ALL sang along. Every last philistine, drugged-out, tracksuit-sporting, ballcap-backwards one of that enormous throng lifted their voices and swayed together for a cold, broken Hallelujah. You could see a moment of surprise flicker across Cohen's giant ancient eagle face on the superscreens before he also gave himself completely to the Song, to the Word. It was strange and unexpected and beautiful. Festivals are like that.

Later that night, back at the circus tent where I was stationed along with a burlesque troop, assorted jugglers, a midget swing band, and a guy who lifted weights with his testicles, Gordon the DJ and I came across a well-dressed man, lying muddy and coma-tose, face-down against our perimeter fence.

We roused him to make sure that he wasn't dead. "Hey, buddy!"

"Hallelujah."

"Saw the Cohen show, didja?"

"Nnnng. Hallelujah."

"You all right there, mate?"

"All right? No I'm not. I'm a corporate head-hunter. I'm just making money for no purpose. I've been wasting my life! I'd rather die than go on as I have."

Festivals are good for that kind of thing.

MANNY AT NORTH COUNTRY FAIR

FESTIVAL! FESTIVAL! FESTIVAL PEOPLE. Ruminating on it, I can't always explain in an easy phrase what it is that makes me continue to work with one specific narcissistic charlatan exhibitionist musician, and drop another. There's just a certain something, a particular characteristic that some of them have, something maybe not charming, but somehow, just compelling, that just keeps me hanging on, as the song says.

For instance ...

I was holding court, as was my wont, at my "office," this Portuguese café on Commercial Drive in Vancouver. The third pitcher of beer had just arrived. With my inimitable, charismatic presence, I authoritatively occupied my usual big round corner window table. There was a small clutch of hangers-on — a few young musicians there who had come for a meeting, hoping to get me to write them a European tour grant application, a young hoping-to-be-a-manager, a grower from the Kootenays I was cultivating as a possible silent partner money-laundering financial backer, and a random drunk nodding off.

And Manny Canoe was in town, from Edmonton. Late thirties, his features still boyish, his brown mop unsalted, unwinnowed, only some crow's feet and that pulled-tight skin from 1980s cocaine abuse as evidence of his age. Financially, he'd had just an average day playing for change on the street, chirping, cooing, and strumming, so he was feeling frustrated, hard-done-by, unappreciated for his genius.

"What about North Country Fair? That's a cool cool festival. Why can't I get back in there? They love me up there! I haven't got in there for, like four, five years. Damn, Cam."

I stretched my lanky Alberta frame and drew breath slowly, in order to draw attention to myself. Preparing to rant, like a Muskox stamping before a charge. I never like to waste any of this display by having my audience miss the beginning.

"Why, Manny? Why can't you get back into North Country Fair?" I asked. "It's so hard to say." I demurred, scratching my five-day-beard chin in theatrical mock puzzlement. "It's a mystery.... Could it be because you arrived four days early for the festival, with no tent, no sleeping bag, and no money, then demanded an advance on your fee, and complained that the beer garden wasn't open yet?

"Could it be that, having been hired as a solo act, you proceeded to form a band out of amateur musicians you'd never met, let alone played with before, and then tried to renegotiate your fee on the basis that you had to take care of your 'people'?"

At this point, Manny attempted to speak, but I of course had anticipated this, and he was no match for my magnetic, authoritative presence while in mid-solo. I silenced him with a broad sweep of my hand that came within a quarter of an inch of actually striking him in the nose, and continued my oration.

"Could it be, Manny, that, having rehearsed your new band once, you then complained to the festival director that your main stage performance was scheduled too early in the evening, because daylight would kill the 'vibe' of the 'project'? This, in a festival that takes place at Summer Solstice, seven hours' drive due north of Edmonton, where the sun actually *does not ever go down?*"

"Twilight! I wanted twilight, I —"

"Could it be the fact that, during your performance, it was plain for all to see, when you pointed your vocal microphone at the moon and urged the crowd to 'Beg her to sing for us!' that you were extremely, violently high on mushrooms? And partly as a result, you played a full fifteen minutes over your allotted time, before you literally had to be wrestled off the stage?

"No, actually, I think it was more likely possibly connected to the series of events after your performance, when you then proceeded to get drunk and take *more* mushrooms with the sixteen-year-old daughter of the festival artistic director, fuck her noisily on the hill leading to the tent area, and stay awake and drunk all the way to your now-legendary 10 a.m. children's stage performance the next day, where you leapt down and led the children, skipping, Pied Piper–style, into an impassable swamp full of nettles. But it's hard to say." I leaned back in my chair. "It's hard to say."

Manny's response demonstrates the reason why, to this day, I still can't help myself from working with him, trying to help him, despite my better judgment. Without taking even a moment for reflection, he blinked once and said, "Well, okay, but that was what, four years ago. Has she heard the new album?"

HERE COMES TEAM FUN

AT ANY RATE, ALTHOUGH MANNY would never have been booked into Calgary on his own, he had enough of a name in folk circles that if I vouched for him and made it clear that he was there as a sideman, Leslie Stark, the artistic director of the Calgary Folk Festival, was willing to tolerate his presence. She has a thing for weird shit, anyway.

I woke when I hit the back of the seat in front of me. I'd been lying lengthwise on the back bench of the minivan, taking a beer-nap.

"Mother fuck!" Jenny shouted.

Mykola was at the wheel, his panicky deep breathing interfering with his attempts to calm us. "It's (*gasp!*) ooookay, everybody (*gasp!*)."

Jenny leaned over to take a look at the speedometer. "One-sixty! In a fucking minivan! You crazy fuck! You slow this thing down!"

"It's (*gasp!*) okay, everyone! Just caaaaalm down. There was a deer or something, but we avoided it, it's long gone now."

Jenny's a person who's mastered that delightful alchemy of conquering fear by instantaneously transmuting it into anger.

"I'll tell you what, I'll fucking punch you in the mouth right now if you don't fucking slow down."

"I think ya better listen to the lady."

Mykola is not tough. Not that way, anyway. He slowed down, pumping the brakes erratically.

"Sorry, everybody, I guess I'm just sorta nervous, excited about this festival, so I wasn't watching the speed. Sorry, sorry."

Jenny relaxed a bit. "Just fucking watch that speed. I don't know what you're in such a fucking rush for, we're probably not even gonna get to play."

I wiped the beery eye-gunk away. "Excuse me?"

"I mean, what the fuck are we gonna do when they figure out that Athena's not coming?"

"Look, I told you, I got that all figured out."

"Yeah, right. I'm beginning to figure out your deal a bit more, Ouiniette. You know, Cole Dixon says he spent Canada Day in a sports bar in Charlottetown that didn't even know he was coming, and he wound up having to buy pitchers for his band, his band that he flew all the way over from fucking England to do the gig. And they didn't even *have* music at that bar anymore!"

"Look, that was a misunderstanding that was actually completely sorted out between me and Cole."

"Oh yeah. He said you demanded a *booking fee* for that gig."

"Well, listen, you're here, aren't you, so unless you have a different plan, let's go with mine."

"Which is what, exactly? They want Athena, not us."

"They don't know what they fucking want. They 'want' good music, as in, they are in a position of 'want' for it, seeing as how their headliners are Great Big C U Next Tuesday and fucking Tom Cochrane. You guys have a hundred times the talent in your fucking little fingers of half the bullshit they've got there. Once they get a load of your amazingness, they'll be in the right frame of mind where we can make it all work. I've done this before. Just trust me."

This emphatic reference to their collective brilliance turned the temperature of the whining down considerably. Flattery is like heroin: people use it because it works.

"Yeah, well, we'll fucking see."

"Cam?"

"What is it, big man?"

"Athena's okay with us going in and using her name for cover to get into the festival, right?"

That was a fair question. You didn't want to make Athena mad. She might have been about five feet tall, but when I went up on the trip North to sign her, her Nova Scotia transplant ex-boyfriend told me he'd seen her single-handedly take down a caribou, dress it, and carry it back to camp seven miles on her back. "She's not vegetarian, but she won't eat what she calls 'southern shit-meat.' Our freezer used to be full of things Theen had killed." He'd confided in me, nostalgically.

"Athena is so far up into the Big Time now, she doesn't give a flying fuck what we do. But, yes she knows what we're doing, and she's totally okay with it. She loves you guys. And she knows she wouldn't have got where she is today without me. Without us."

That seemed to do it.

"I'm just excited to get to play such a big folk festival. And Jimmy Kinnock is kind of my hero since I was a kid, and —"

"Yeah, well don't get so excited that you crash us off the side of a mountain."

The girl had a point there. An average of one band per year dies driving Canada's Highway 1 over the Rocky Mountains, through Rogers Pass. You're like to get smoked by a logging truck skidding over the yellow line, or if you slip and go off the side there, you better pack a lunch because you'll get hungry on the fall down.

APOLOGY FOR DIGRESSION

DAMN, I WAS SCRIBBLING AWAY HERE, and I was having trouble seeing what I was writing. I started to worry if maybe I was going blind, but then I looked up round me in this dilapidated kitchen and realized that the sun was going down. My ass and back hurt from being bent over scrawling, and this poor old kitchen table is full of defaced yellow legal paper. Also, I was dimly aware of myself picking with my fingernails at the flaking baby-blue paint on the table top, but I now see that someone seems to have stripped the entire table to bare pine, and there's paint flakes everywhere. Don't see anybody else here so I guess that was me. I remember promising to only write a dozen pages or so, just the bare bones of the story of what happened at the Calgary Folk Festival, and here I am at twenty or more and I haven't even got us to the festival. Sorry about that, reader, but what can you do? There's stuff people need to know, in order to understand what an extraordinary figure I am, and what it is I do for people. Sometimes a digression or two is necessary, and I'm not sorry. Genius works in mysterious ways. If I had more time, I'd try to winnow the thing down, but I think it's a better idea to just take a short break, get some candles lit, eat a tomato, do some more speed, take a shot of whiskey, and get back down to business. If a job's worth doing, I always say, it's worth doing half-assed, so long as it gets done.

ARRIVAL: COWTOWN

RIGHT. I'M BACK AT 'ER. Got my writing hat on. Let's cut straight to Calgary.

Nobody has ever called Calgary a pretty city. "The big city with the small town feel" is the slogan that boosters like to cite, and for once, the P.R. guys aren't lying. Calgary is big, and it's getting bigger all the time. The people who run Calgary would give Jane Jacobs an aneurysm, if they ever met her, but they don't run in the same circles. Calgary believes in '50s-style suburban-development sprawl. If you see it from the air at night, its lights and grid make it look exactly like a massive Pac-Man game laid out flat on the dark screen of the prairie, and the high price of oil is making it ever-expanding, like a flood, but a flood of garbage. When we passed the city-limit marker, I noticed the green-and-white sign was mounted on a John Deere lawnmower, trundling west along the shoulder of the highway at five miles per hour. There's eight of these lawnmowers, constantly moving outward from Calgary at every point of the compass.

Small-town feel? Absolutely. If you think of small towns as places full of small-minded people who mistrust racial minorities and single mothers, where the downtown turns into a ghost town at 5 p.m., then yesiree, Calgary's got it, by gum. Only lucky thing about Calgary is that the lefty weirdo people can't be laid-back and pathetically over-confident, like in Vancouver. Calgary oddballs have to huddle together against the storm of SUV materialism and shitty New Country music.

So as we pulled into the Westin Hotel in Renty the rental minivan, I naturally took the attitude of a regiment of cavalry, coming to relieve a besieged holdout. Triumphant, swaggering, cheerful, task-oriented. I drank a couple Red Bulls as Jenny swore us through the midday downtown traffic. I had to have the cheerful nonchalance of a busy man with nothing to hide and nothing on his mind except Achievement.

I told Jenny to guard the gear and Manny, and dragged the Fat Boy along with me to keep him from wandering off. Mykola is always wandering off, either daydreaming a song and forgetting where he is, or just chasing pussy, which he is surprisingly good at. Just off the lobby was a meeting room with a Jiffy Marker sign that said "Artist Registration, Liaison and Transportation." I marched in.

A friendly looking late-middle-aged chubby lesbian in a festival sweatshirt and bifocals was at the folding table, where the piles of artist envelopes sat.

"Well hello there, sir!"

"Well hello there yoursleff, ma'am. I'm here to register Athena Amarok."

She smiled, "Okey dokey ..." and started ticking her fingers over the envelopes, checking names through the bottom of the bifocals.

"And you are?"

"Cam Ouiniette. Manager."

"So I'll tick her off then."

She handed me the envelope. I checked that it had passes, drink tickets, and meal vouchers for everybody in the band.

"Do you know if Jimmy Kinnock's manager, Richard Wren, is around nearby? Has he collected his package recently?"

"Sorry, no. They haven't checked in yet. I'm really looking forward to his set tomorrow, though. I'd crawl over broken glass for that man."

"Me, too. Listen, I was wondering, Athena's playing Sunday night, so she's sure to be *exhausted* after her show. Could we take care of the money at this point, so we don't have to futz around with it when everybody's tired and everything?"

"The money?" She sounded surprised that there was money somehow involved in this wonderful party she was helping to throw. Volunteers.

"Yes, can we grab the cheque here?"

"Oh, well, I believe it's Sheryl who takes care of the money." Pause.

"Is she around?"

"Umm ... no, she doesn't seem to be about."

"Can you get her on the walkie-talkie?"

"Is Ms. Amarok here? I believe she needs to sign the invoice for that."

"She'll be arriving shortly. I have proxy to sign for her. I'm the Manager."

"Well, I dunno if Sheryl is on shift right now."

Suddenly, from behind, I heard a sharp, theatrical intake of breath, and a dropping of a guitar.

"Eyah! I'm not going in there!"

"What's the matter, Colleen? Are you alright?"

Oh, man. I'd forgotten She was coming.

"I'm not going in there with that *rapist*."

I turned and took quick action to defend my name. "Lady, if you're going to make accusations, you better be prepared to back them up. I demand that you call the cops and have me arrested, if you're going to bandy that word about in relation to me."

Colleen's heaving breathing began to accelerate, like someone giving birth. "What you did to me was a *violation*."

Her handler, a lady in a bulky old Cowichan sweater, took her arm, soothingly. The lesbian at the desk was suddenly not so friendly-looking any more. She used the upper half of her bifocals now to attempt to peer into my soul to see if this new portrait of me was correct. I tried to explain to the room.

"I'm her ex-Manager. A lot of artists feel that way about their managers. Believe me, the feeling is mutual on my part."

"You fucked me. You fucked me! I'm not going in there with that fucking fucking *monster!*" Thank God. Colleen's screaming profanity was bringing down the general estimation of her sanity in the room full of conflict-averse Canadians.

The desk lady looked at me, authoritatively. "Have you got all your passes and everything? Maybe you can come back another time and deal with the cheque stuff. Alright, *sir?*" Yikes.

"Listen, I just want to quickly —"

"He trapped me in a gunfight! He put me in a *war zone!* He was directly responsible for almost killing me!"

I handed Mykola the envelopes and his face showed that he had clearly taken another step in his long journey of reassessing me as his ticket to the Big Time.

"Come on, let's go. I have no interest in having a conversation with this person."

"Nor do I!" shouted Colleen. She shrank back from us, shielding her face as we passed as if I were emanating a visible toxin.

WE WERE NOT TRAPPED

FOR COLLEEN TO SAY "you trapped me in the Siege of Sarajevo" in that way of hers, narrowing her eyes and shooting accusative 1980s feminist separatist death rays at me, it's totally unfair. And inaccurate. We weren't trapped, and we weren't in Sarajevo, exactly. Anyway, I saved her life, and you would think I would get some gratitude for it, but she always had to emphasize the idea that I was responsible for putting her life in danger in the first place. Negativity. That's what that is. Negativity.

You have to remember, before the shit all went down, Sarajevo was a *normal fucking place!* They'd just had the *Olympics* there, for Chrissakes. It had more (and better) newspapers than Toronto, and a better music scene, too. Cosmopolitan. Szechuan restaurants. Avant-garde installation art in the square. Muslims, Croats, Serbs, Jews, Albanians, Gypsies, Macedonians, all living *normally*. No big deal. I mean, the airport was still open, you know. I guess there was some kind of travel advisory or something, but they put that kind of thing out every time some elderly tourist gets a new strain of the flu or whatever, so you can't live your life by that kind of thing.

Of course there was tension, I knew that, but I rarely read the papers, and I had great contacts on the ground, some extremely interesting experimental noise musicians. Made a sound like having your face run over by the street cleaner at six in the morning at the end of an acid trip. Fabulous. And of course as soon as they heard Colleen, they went *apeshit* about her. They *had* to have her over. And they were eminently suggestible to anything else I had in mind. So that's how I came to put on a seven-band Canadian Music Weakness Festival that, it turned out, took place at the start of the Yugoslavian Civil War. Entirely funded by Canadian tax payer money, I'll have you know, thanks to Yours Truly.*

---

* You're probably not interested, unless you're hoping to go into the music business yourself, but here's the thing about Canadian music grants, especially this organization called FACRAL (The Foundation to Assist Canadian Records and Licensees): They're designed as a subsidy for the music business, not as a way to help musicians. That's an important distinction. They're a back-door giveaway of money that's not supposed to go to people who really need it, but to people in the Music Biz Establishment. People like Sarah McLachlan's managers dipped into that dough forever, from their houses in Shaughnessy. The bureaucrats deliberately set up the criteria as best they can to keep independent types like the kind I work with out of their trough. But almost none of the bureaucrats have ever been on tour, or run anything in the actual music world. They just toodle around on the government dime, seeing shows for free and jerking each other off at conferences and the like. They don't actually have a clue how it all really works, so they're laughably easy to fool. So for the last fifteen years, me and them have played a game of cat-and-mouse, where I find tricky ways to meet the letter of their fucked-up criteria (mostly under assumed names), and then when they realize how much money they've handed to a bunch of people they've never heard of, they revise the criteria again to keep the riff-raff out. And then I figure out a way to beat it. They say, "You must have national distribution to apply." So I smoke up some guy from a distributor of toasters and talk him into putting my grunge band's cassette in his catalogue. Then the next year they say, "You have to have shipped this many albums." So I pay a couple hundred bucks to ship 'em from Vancouver to Innisfail, and trigger a $15,000 grant. Then the next year they say, "You have to have sold this many records." So I purchase that many albums from the toaster guy, get the grant, and sell the albums again back to the band. It's a process, like I say. But it really was my greatest coup ever to get FACRAL to inadvertently fund an entire music festival in Yugoslavia at the moment of that nation's demise. Of course, there was a price to be paid after that. They *really* tightened up the rules after they looked at their end-of-year receipts and saw how many of them were in Serbo-Croatian. I've heard that any time Ivy Easton-Day at FACRAL hears someone speak my name, her eyeballs literally spurt blood.

Colleen is the perfect example of a musician who is too good for their own good. *Too* powerful. *Too* charismatic. She takes people *too* far into the emotions of the music. Sometimes they never get out. There was that joke band Spinal Tap that had all their dead drummers, but I know of at least three of Colleen's ex-drummers who have signed their own papers to be committed to the nuthouse. No, I am not exaggerating. Certainly, many who've played with her never pick up an instrument again, myself included. It just doesn't help your career to be that good.

For instance, the time I got her the opening slot on one of the early Sarah McLachlan tours. Sarah the Pretty Guitar-Strumming Tree Nymph was just starting to take off, already drawing packed houses at the biggest university bars across the country. So it was a good gig. But it couldn't last.

The problem was, Colleen, somewhat dumpy, bespectacled, patchy-thrift-store-dressed Colleen, would step quietly up to the mic in her dead abusive stepfather's parade boots, plug her pawnshop electric guitar *into the PA*, no fancy amplifier necessary, and simply *destroy-and-simultaneously-rebuild people's minds*, like if an ice pick to your cortex did the opposite of a lobotomy.

By the last song, the audience was so in thrall to her dark powers that it was nothing, a mere *bagatelle*, for her to ask for two random white male volunteers from the crowd to don Lone Ranger masks, strip naked on stage and smash beer bottles into an oil drum that we travelled with. She liked to make them flank her and cavort devilishly to the rhythm of the final, heart-rending song about the lonely death of her half brother in the Medicine Hat municipal jail.

I used to love to watch the audience slowly file out of the bar at the break, panicky, stunned, emotionally exhausted, mouths hanging open, eyes darting to-and-fro, like dogs after Halloween fireworks.

Needless to say, the vampires at Nettwerk Music (who are both management and record label, a felony in most countries, just by the way) kicked her off the tour after three shows. Can't have Sarah the Neo-Raphaelite Tree Nymph getting shown up every night by some weird lady who looks like a washerwoman but has ten times the talent.

But I digress. Back to the war …

When I landed at Sarajevo airport with Colleen, her band, and an assortment of other Canucks, all seemed fine. We were greeted by Bobo, my old friend who was a TV journalist at the time. But no cameras. "Where's the cameras?" I asked, a bit annoyed. I like a bit of publicity.

"Busy covering something else …" He waved vaguely. I could see that he was drunk, which was not remarkable. I was mainly concerned with the labour-intensive job of keeping Colleen not wholly unhappy, but she started flirting aggressively with Bobo, so that kept her too busy to find a reason to get mad at me, so I wasn't too worried about anything, to be honest.

Of course, the "something else" Bobo was referring to turned out to be the fucking Yugoslav National Army shooting a bunch of women on a peace march in downtown Sarajevo, and things just kinda went downhill from there, as history records.

I knew none of this at the time, and Bobo wasn't really talking much. He had had such high naive hopes for the peace march, he had dropped acid to heighten the anticipated experience of Triumphant People Power, so the gunfire and the blood and corpses and screaming and everything had kind of harshed out his trip, to say the least. He insisted we all go to his favourite underground bar and have a bunch of beer and hash and sausage and *Loza* moonshine, and since that's what I always traditionally do to combat jet lag, I noticed no interruption of normal conditions, and no reason to break precedent.

Now you will say that I was responsible for all those people, and that at that moment of crisis, I should have known to keep a clear head, to take the situation more seriously. But honestly, everyone who came to that festival was an adult, ultimately responsible for their own lives, their own choices. And they all managed to survive, and the only one who got shot was the keyboard player in that crummy Goth band, and only because he suddenly decided to remember that he was a Croat, and that he needed to fight for the Old Cause that his stupid grandmother had been feeding him lies about, raising him up in fucking Norval, Ontario, which is a town that is a Crime Against Humanity in and of itself, if you've never been there, believe me. And that is not my fault.

At this point in the narrative, my recollection naturally becomes somewhat blurred, on account of the beer, the hash, the *Loza*, and — always wanting to be sociable with local customs — the acid I naturally dropped when Bobo offered it to me.

I remember a great party, and then this rumbling sound, which must have been shells falling, but at the time sounded like ravenous monsters coming to eat us, especially when the lights went off. Then I remember a lot of running and screaming in the dark, and that seemed to go on for several lifetimes. But I guess that because of growing up on a ranch, I've always had a little bit of sheepdog in me, and somehow I managed to keep us together, the core group of Colleen, me, Steve the bass player, and Nellis the drummer. I think the guitar player found a woman somewhere along the way.

When I phased back to consciousness, we were all crouched in a stairwell on the outside of a large grey concrete building. It was raining lightly. I think that the sun had just come up. I heard the sound of stray rifle ricochets, but they were coming from at least a few streets away, which I take as proof that my powers of crisis management must have been working even when my mind was locked in the acid-and-moonshine blackout.

I surveyed my people. Steve the bass player was staring at the grey concrete wall in front of him, immobile. From the rhythmic movement of his lips, he seemed to be singing something, but he wasn't making any sound. Anyway, he wasn't going anywhere, so that was alright. As for the drummer, you can always count on them to just keep compulsively tap-tap-tapping on whatever's in front of them, no matter what's going on, and Nellis was no exception as, red-eyed, his dirty purple hair stringy from old sweat, he twitchingly practised his paradiddles with his index fingers pinging on the iron railing.

I looked over at Colleen. She was crouched, with her back to me. Her body was shuddering, and she was sniffling violently. We'd been more than manager/client for some time, and her sniffling awoke my tender feelings for her. I thought of the wonderful times we'd had, breaking into the mink farms in rural Netherlands, setting the angry little animals free, and the night we spent in jail when she attacked an airport security guard in Copenhagen with her guitar case, screaming the word "Nazi!" at him over and over. She really was wonderful in her own fucked-up way. I went over to comfort her, but when she turned around it became clear that she was not crying at all, but had just been hacking up a big yellow loogie, which she proceeded to spit directly onto the toe of my cowboy boot.

She gave me that *look* she has, and enunciated very clearly, "I am *never* going to let you *fuck me, ever again.*"

This was a drag, since, as I say, we had had a "relationship" for quite some time at that point, and I was very fond of her, in a terrified kind of way. Still, I had never thought that was going to last forever, given Colleen's temper, which linked to her tendency to fall out angrily with pretty much everybody, and then of course there was her rapacious and wide-ranging sexual appetite …

Anyway, I filed the "Love Affair with Colleen: Over" information away as something to Think About Later, and started peering around for a defensible next move. You can't live in a stairwell. Also, I had noticed that the concrete dust and mould was making the drummer's allergies act up. I notice those kinds of things. I always take care of my people.

Then, like a gift from, well, *somebody*, I spotted Marko. Or rather, I didn't know Marko yet, but I saw him, and decided that I intended to know him.

A battered white cube van had pulled up outside a grey, nondescript building similar to our own, across the street and a block and a half away.

I've always had killer eyes, since my Old Pap used to take me hunting prairie dogs and badgers with a .22 when I was five years old. My vision remains considerably better than 20/20, although I sometimes wear transparent eyeglasses in heavy negotiations, for the sake of intellectual intimidation.

So it was easy for me to pick out, on the back of the black T-shirt of the dreadlocked headbanger who got out of the van, the symbol of a very obscure Finnish band, premier practitioners in Finland of a very specialized form of heavy metal called Goat Metal, so-called because the final mix of each track on a Goat Metal album is celebrated by the ritual slaughter and burning of a black goat. The name of the band is of course, Keskonen Suoli, which translates, roughly, as "The Intestines of a Prematurely Born Infant," and I had been a fan since their first classic album, *Nisä Thelema*, or "The Breasts of Thelema," a reference to the writings of that fabulous old Satanist, Aleister Crowley.

My heart leapt like a kid on a griddle. This guy was a rocker who loved one of my favourite bands, and he had a van. I ran toward him, shouting, alternately "Hey! *Keskonen! Keskonen!*" and *"Kaivos Emätin!"* ("Vagina Mining.") "Kaivos Emätin" was a track that appeared only on the original Estonian vinyl pressing of the album. I wanted him to know that I wasn't just a superficial dilettante Keskonen fan.

I guess my Finnish pronunciation wasn't so hot, and after being up for forty-eight hours, counting the plane ride, and also being all covered in plaster dust and other debris, maybe I looked a bit threatening, because the headbanger saw me and made a panicky break for it, abandoning his van. I jumped in it to find the keys in the ignition and the engine still running. I threw it in gear and gave chase, leaning my torso out the window and shouting the name of the deleted album track at the top of my voice as I drove just behind him. It took a whole city block for him to finally get the point that I wasn't some crazed Serb out to murder him.

"*Keskonen! 'Kaivos Emätin!' Keskonen!*" I was waving the secret Ronnie James Dio rock 'n' roll devil horns at him with my right hand, pumping it enthusiastically above my head. "You know?"

I watched a look of puzzlement cross his face, and then the penny dropped. He stopped. His face lit up. "*Keskonen! Keskonen Suoli?*"

"Right!" I stopped the van and jumped out, still holding up my devil horns.

"*Nisä Thelema?*"

"Yes! You got it, buddy!"

He frowned thoughtfully, pushed his dreads out of his face, looked me right in the eyes, and spoke: "I must say that I don't like that one as much as the third album, the self-titled one. Talk about a band's true statement. That is the real deal, that one. Mindblowing." That's the thing with Scandinavians — because they generally speak better English than we do, their grasp of the idiom can actually be a bit disconcerting at times.

As if in response to the man's carefully considered and totally wrongheaded statement, the stray *zings* of the ricochets started noticeably ramping up in volume. But there was no way that I was going to let such an outrage pass without comment.

"That's ludicrous. The third album was a completely obvious, commercial bid for crossover into mainstream speed metal."

"Commercial? Please. They couldn't even play their instruments properly on their first album. Even those who are deaf can hear it in the first bar of the first track!"

Even those who are deaf would have been able to discern the unmistakably solid, dependable sound of AK-47s approaching.

"No way, that's youthful energy. The guitarist's mother was a concert pianist. You can't tell me they didn't know how to play."

We both cringed involuntarily as an artillery shell screamed, what seemed like inches overhead. The headbanger waited for the explosion in the next neighbourhood over before he made his point.

As he grabbed my arm and pulled me into the van, he shouted, "She wasn't a concert pianist, I knew the family. She was an amateur light opera singer, and not a very good one, at that. You'd better come with me — I want you to listen to track six, the first track on the second side of the vinyl."

So that's how, thanks to my interest in Satanic Metal, we found ourselves drinking forty-year-old wine from Czech crystal in a beautiful chateau overlooking a beautiful city burning beautifully, listening to records on a first-rate stereo with beautiful warm old Soviet vacuum-tube amplification, safe as could reasonably be demanded, under the circumstances. Turns out Marko was in Sarajevo because his girlfriend was a Bosnian Muslim. Her uncle was some kind of businessman with links to Albania, and he had this skookum joint on the hillside.

Marko's girlfriend took Colleen off to show her the bath. I couldn't be sure, but as she walked away, she (not Colleen, but Marko's girlfriend) seemed to be kind of looking at me funny, like I had a bug on my head or something. When women find me attractive I never look for an explanation, I just go with it. I wasn't sure that was what the look meant, though. Reading women's desires is kind of my one social Achilles heel in my charm juggernaut.

Nellis was a big fan of expensive booze, so he was keeping himself busy trying different vintages. The uncle had brought his best bottles up from the cellar, working from the sound principle that when the country's falling apart, you might as well drink the good stuff now. I decided to tangibly endorse that principle, with vigour.

Steve still wasn't speaking audibly, just doing that silent lip-moving thing, but I did manage to get some wine in him, and I put on Neil Young's version of "Four Strong Winds," kinda the Western Canadian national anthem. It seemed to calm him down.

"Steve, look at me," I said, summoning my best Certainty Tone. I raised my right hand, two forefingers together at my forehead. "I swear, Scout's Honour, I'm gonna get us all home safe and sound. I promise. You can take that to the bank."

He just stared down at the city as the shells pinged off bits of the taller buildings in the centre. He was weeping, softly singing, "Think I'll go out to Alberta, weather's good there in the fall ..."

FRIDAY NIGHT, WESTIN HOTEL

SURVEYING CALGARY'S ARID SKYLINE of oil-money office towers from the window of the eighteenth floor of the Westin, I cracked open the tiny bottle of wine in the cute wicker basket and drained it in a swallow. A corner of Prince's Island Park, where the festival takes place each year, was visible in the lower right corner, like a small green attempt at a backhanded apology for the rest of the dystopic beige city. Manny had already buggered off to jam with some Iranian Reggae band or something, but Mykola and Jenny were standing in the doorway of the hotel room, asking me skeptical questions about petty logistics. Luckily, I have a remarkably strong ability to ignore things that I don't want to pay attention to, so I managed to tune them out completely, in order to contemplate the overall situation and the status of my strategy for the weekend. I lit a cigarette.

As much as I had successfully parried Colleen's accusations, it was obvious that the festival check-in had resulted in, overall, a strategically mixed outcome. It was essential that I extract the full fee for Athena's performance as soon as possible, before Leslie Stark, the director of the festival, figured out that Athena wasn't coming. There was no way I would get Leslie herself to agree to paying out before the performance, so I had to find some unwary underling with cheque-signing authority to take care of it, meanwhile avoiding Leslie for as long as possible, because Leslie is sharp. Yikes.

PORTRAIT OF LESLIE STARK WITH THE AUSTRALIAN SINGER-SONGWRITER

LESLIE STARK IS ONE OF THE BEST of the A.D.s, because she actually has extraordinarily good, far-ranging taste in music. Runs some kind of unlistenable experimental jazz show on the university radio station. I like her 'cause she gets bored easy, and she doesn't have the social skills to hide it. She's almost autistic in her ability to obtusely trample people's feelings. A lot of people — hippies, especially — can't handle her. She traumatizes them.

My favourite story about Leslie to illustrate her hilarious insensitivity is about this awful Australian singer-songwriter who was in Canada, trying to build an audience here on the folk circuit.

First of all, you may call me "prejudiced," you may think I'm not "politically correct," but I have a right to my opinions, and I personally feel that Australians are subhuman. Not the Aborigines of course, I mean the blond ones that surf or whatever. They have a kind of easy friendliness that reminds me of Californians, but worse. My favourite peoples in the world are the Finns, the Czechs, and the Bosnians. These are sullen, melancholy, suspicious people who are extremely difficult to impress. Australians will call you their "mate" within the first five seconds of meeting you. I despise that. If a Czech decides that he's your friend, he'll fucking die for you. But you have to *earn* his friendship and respect, over a period of *years*. He will not hug you. Australian friendship, like their culture, goes about an inch deep. Don't mistake their blond bounciness for the stupid but endearing loyalty of the Golden Retriever. No. At their core, they're like cats — once you leave the room, they've forgotten you exist, and they're thinking about lunch. And their songwriting is like that. An Australian lyricist is aiming, with her words, for a kind of McCartney-esque mellifluousness, like the waves crashing soothingly, mindlessly, repetitively, on the beach. They've never met a cliché that they didn't like. Australian songs are full of lyrics like

"I feel like I live in a mind of my own
And all I can learn is all that I've known."

Or

"Runaway train, gonna run all night,
Got on board this ev'nin' and I'll be there by daylight."

Or

"We can change the shape of the world, just by seeing from a
different point of view!"

Not that there aren't Canadian songs that are just as awful. But for Australia, apart from Nick Cave, *that's all they've got.*

So this Australian chick has been campaigning for a year and a half to get into Leslie's festival. Demo CDs with scented candles, recycled-paper bags of home-baked muffins, weekly emails, monthly phone calls. Leslie listens to half of one song, with its lyric about how we need to love our Mother, and our Mother is Mother Nature, or how it's Lonely Out On the Road, or something, and writes her off.

But the Ozesse persists. She "networks" with other Canadian singer-songwriters, pressuring *them* to ask Leslie to *"give her a chance"* and at least go see her play live.

So finally, Leslie gets sick of this and takes the situation in hand. She goes out to the little café where the Australian is the featured performer at the open-mic night. After she's done, the chick goes straight to Leslie's table to start lobbying for the festival gig.

Leslie responds, "You aren't ready to play the festival."

"Yes I am! I am ready. Why not?"

Others would hem and haw. Others would put her off with promises of "maybe next year." Not Leslie. She just smiles and lets her have it, point blank. "Your singing is just okay, you can barely play guitar, and all that wouldn't be such an issue, but your songwriting is intensely unoriginal. You're just very unoriginal."

You've got to give the girl credit. She doesn't quit. Like a cheerful young piece of cannon fodder at Gallipoli, she continues charging, undaunted, into the unconquerable heavy guns of the enemy — to get her empty head blown off.

"No, I'm not unoriginal. That's so unfair! I'm actually very … original."

At this point, Leslie offers the *coup de grace*. She fishes into her purse and hands the girl a pass to the festival in July.

"Here, come to the festival, and listen to some of the acts that play there. That'll give you an idea of how good you'd have to be to get in as a performer." And she walks away. Wow. What a woman. I really needed to stay away from her till Sunday, or the jig could be up.

PURPOSEFUL MARCH TO THE FESTIVAL

I NEEDED SOME FRESH AIR and a break from my musicians, so I donned the fresh white terry-cloth hotel bathrobe and made ready to head down to the lobby and the short walk to the festival site. Mykola and Jenny waved their arms, trying to get me to answer their concerns, but as I had no idea what they'd been saying for the last ten minutes, I merely shouted something like, "You're free on shore leave till the workshop at 2 p.m. tomorrow. Be there a half-hour before. Make sure you've got something figgered out by then if you know what's good for ya" and then headed out to the elevators.

There's something about wearing a good bathrobe out in public that I've always enjoyed. Just the right balance between Rasputin-like madness and regal authority.

In the lobby, the famous and semi-famous were arriving in the festival shuttle cargo vans, with their flight cases and their jet-lagged, need-a-shower-and-a-shave-and-a-shit faces. I really could have used some sleep (and maybe a long bath, I guess) myself, but it was up to me as Manager to go out and Represent and Network and buy people beers with other people's money and enlighten the ignorant as to my many unique and valuable opinions. Heads were turned by the sheer energy that I emanated as I marched briskly and purposefully toward the revolving doors. But once I'd parsed the faces to make sure there was no Richard Wren among them, I only spared them a few random R.A.F.-style salutes and tips of my imaginary hat as I strode. It was festival time.

I love the walk to the festival, whether from the hotel or the parking area or wherever. I like to feel the excitement building in the audience as they make their way toward the gates. They chatter to each other, carrying their blankets and camping gear and extra layers for the chill when the sun goes down. For a lot of these people, this one weekend is the highlight of their entire year, when they see old pals who moved away and maybe only come back to town for Folk Fest, when they cut loose a little (or a lot), when they find the music they're going to be listening to on their joe-job commutes for the rest of the year, the music that will give them the spiritual strength to get up in the dark of a Canadian morning and drag themselves into another workday that no matter how deadening, at least takes them a day closer to the next Folk Fest.

They moved in little clumps of family and friends, usually somebody reading a program as they walked, figuring out what they wanted to see this weekend, what they'd heard of, what "looks interesting."

It did my heart good to see one clump that appeared to be three generations of counter-culture types: an elderly Beat-professor type Grampa, a couple of middle-aged Deadheads, and a teenaged punk son, all sharing a nasty-sweet-smelling joint as they meandered along. I asked them for a hit, and they shared it with me in the true spirit of Alberta horse brutality.

Then we got to the giant opening night lineup, and the counter-cultural dopehead family stopped at the back of the three-block-long queue, and it did my heart good to breeze past them, fingering my backstage pass as they slumped in resignation for the long, boring wait ahead of them. Berner the lying Jew accordionist likes to wear a linen suit and a panama hat with mirrored shades for just these moments, when he can pretend to be a Caribbean plantation owner, surveying his "crop" of new audience. That's taking the joke a little too far, a tendency he can never resist, but still, his un-Christian inability to feel shame in his pleasures is one of the ways that he and I intersect.

My ears were pricked by a sound coming up from near the gate. Too loud to be a faraway stage. There was something musical happening.

It was revealed to be a cute young ragamuffin jug band of five squeegee punks, playing a skooching fast hillbilly tune on some thrift-store acoustic instruments. First thing I noticed was the fiddle. It keened high above the other stuff that chuckered along. The big dirty tattooed pierced banjo guy with electrical-taped glasses was singing, and the fiddle would talk back at each of his phrases, rapid-fire, like your favourite drinking buddy who knows how to make your jokes funnier as you tell them. The fiddler was a little guy in a ripped black leather jacket, wearing a dark blue Lucky Lager cap. You couldn't see his face under the brim, 'cause it was bent down looking at the banjo player's hands. He was simultaneously leaning into a tough-looking, pretty girl playing gutbucket one-string bass, absorbing the beat through his back. Boy that fiddle kid could play. Play fast, ripping notes off with the gliss of an expert pickpocket. Play slow, lovely little ornaments on the melody, never losing the pitch except accidentally-on-purpose for emphasis, to tell you something about the jumbled way the music was making him feel. How old was he? He was barely over five feet tall. Was he some kind of tweenage runaway from fucking Julliard, dragging his classical chops through the mud?

The song itself emerged from the din, and it clarified as a cover of "Gin & Juice" by Snoop Dogg. "Got my mind on my money and my money on my mind," a good choice to underline the falseness of trying to separate White Music and Black Music in the history of American Music. Most of the audience of lineup people were digging it, and coins were falling in the guitar case. A handsome, skinny guitarist boy in a crushed top hat was on his back next to the case, rolling around and strumming up at the punette girl guitar player, who I noticed had a black sling on her back with a sleeping baby in it. The little nipper sported a skull-and-crossbones baby cap. A cardboard sign propped up against the fence read "The Supersonic Ramblers! Donations Xepted!"

The song skittered and spun to a halt like a NASCAR wall-collision accident, and the lineup applauded. The little fiddler lifted up his head and smiled a weird, pointy-toothed smile, and of course it was a girl! How dumb of me. No boy could play like that, with that kind of sophistication of feeling. Well, maybe if you kept him at the bottom of a well for a year or something.

"Nice one," I said as I tossed a five-dollar bill in the guitar case.

"Thank you!" said the girl fiddler, and she smiled again. It looked like the teeth on either side of her canines had been pulled or knocked out. It made her look like some kind of feral rodent, or a wolverine or something. But the full force of her happiness at the way they'd played the song, the gladness about getting the fiver, it sort of blazed out at you. It won you over to her side of things, right away. It was strange, like her playing.

"Hey, mister," said the girl with the baby on her back. "I see you gotta backstage pass. You somebody important or something?"

"You have no idea how important," I responded.

This didn't faze her. "Well, then, can you get us in past the gates? They won't let us in. We'd make way more cash on the inside."

"Don't be so sure, kid. Keep playing!" I shot that back over my shoulder as I pushed on past the security volunteers, waving the pass.

THE REST OF THE EVENING I was on a kind of drunk, tired automatic pilot, just working the exhaustion and the road out of my shoulders, drinking in the backstage, mostly not listening to the main-stage acts. I was wrung out by the ten-hour drive from Vancouver, and sometimes I find the collegial, familiar atmosphere of the beer garden soothing. The folk festival circuit is kind of a travelling small town, where the same performers and tech people see each other weekend after weekend. For the host city itself, the festival appears only once a year, like Brigadoon, but for the people behind the curtain, there's a comforting weekly sameness to the Drinks Tent, no matter which city or town it might be located in this week. Same plastic chairs, same plastic tables sporting plastic beer company logo giant parasols, same brutalized yellow-brown beer-soaked grass under your toes, and the chattering sound of the slow release of show-adrenaline, comparisons of tour itineraries, swapped stories of bad behaviour, bad luck, bad hospitality from Timbuktu to Sudbury, et cetera. Comforting old jokes, stray conversation ...

"It's an okay gig, but no good for publicity. Uncle Thirsty says playing that place is like pissing yerself in a dark suit — you get a warm feeling but nobody notices."

"... I said 'that's why they call it a guarantee, 'cause it's *guaranteed,* arschloch!' So he says they just don't have the money, so then I said, 'Well, this microphone looks like it cost five hundred euros, if you ain't got the cash, I'll just take this.'"

"Anyway, later I'm lying there, and suddenly he sits up, and he says, 'You know what? I like you. So you know what I'm gonna do for you?'"

At the table next to me, Rosalyn Knight, the boozy country chanteuse, was cackling merrily, with her customary Du Maurier cigarette in one hand, glass of red wine in the other. Her crow-black hair fell careless and fetchingly over her somewhat hooky nose. I heard a rumour she's half-Jewess and it doesn't surprise me in the least. She's got the gift of the gab, all right. Plus it's kinda suspicious that someone who's supposed to be a country singer would have so many minor key songs in her repertoire.

"What?"

"He says, 'You know what I'm gonna do? I'm gonna go and wash my penis.'"

"Oh my God! No!"

"Yeah. Kind of a mood killer."

"What'd you say?"

"Nothing. He went off to the can and I made a run for it. Shwip. Gone."

"Wow. Good for you."

"Yeah, he was pretty cute, but his band kinda sucked. They still cover 'Ring of Fire.' Every time somebody plays that song, a little angel loses its wings."

"Where was that? Toronto?"

"You called it! They really know how to treat a lady out there."

"Weren't you just up North too? Get up to anything there? There's a lot of lonely men up there, not many ladies, I hear."

"Please. I mean, the odds are good, but the goods are *odd*, if you know what I mean." More cackling. "Nothing is free, my friend. Nothing is free. Remember that."

My old pal Dugg Simpson, the artistic director of the Vancouver Folk Fest, was sitting with a couple of other A.D.s. These people *get paid* to go and check out each others' festivals. Nobody ever quits that job. It's too good. You either die or get fired. I gotta get me a job like that someday.... Anyway, he looked relaxed and satisfied with himself, so I decided to try to bait him into an argument of some kind.

"You know what the problem is, you've got all this fake 'gypsy' shit played by fucking jazz college kids from fucking Vancouver or Toronto or New England or whatever. Gypsy Jazz. Gypsy Punk. Pretty white Pentecostal girls who ran away from home to play old-time country and write songs about how they're Gypsies. And meanwhile the real Gypsies are back starving in Eastern Europe, 'cause you fuckers are too lazy to jump through the hoops to get them a visa to come here."

"Getting a visa is not a matter of jumping a couple of hoops, Cam! You should know that. The Canadian government will *not* be convinced that these guys aren't coming in order to stay and go on welfare, like immediately."

"Let them go on welfare!" I was starting to roll. "It would be an immeasurable enrichment of Canadian culture to have a few hundred thousand Gypsies over here, on welfare. Besides, nobody works harder than the Roma, and that's a fact. I just can't believe you're booking some asshole from some indie rock band who just discovered this music last summer while he was backpacking, rather than the real deal. Like this band I found in Romania, the Changa Band. I could get them for you — they'll fucking give you a conniption! You'll never book that college boy bullshit again."

"I'm never booking the Changa Band again, that's who I'm never booking again." Dugg crossed his arms.

"You booked them? When?"

"Nine years ago, before *you'd* ever heard of them, boyo. Never again."

"What happened?"

"I paid them a huge fee. In euros. And I got a grant to pay for their flights, went through like, nine months of visa bullshit to get them here. They come to the festival, and they start *busking.*"

"Well, that's what they do, they play. They play on the street, they play wherever. They're fucking Gypsies, man."

"I've got six outdoor stages going simultaneously, each where I try to keep the music sonically separated so there's not too much bleed, and all day Saturday, people are trying to do their concerts, workshops on the stages, what have you, and then the bloody Changas come through, dancing along, playing, and steal the fucking audience like the Pied fucking Piper."

"Well, fair's fair. The audience just liked them more, 'cause they're the real deal. They're geniuses, man."

"Yeah, well my audience has paid, like seventy bucks a head *per day* to come into this festival, and these jokers finish a song, and start *passing the hat* around, literally begging for money."

"Busking! Just 'cause they pass the hat around doesn't mean they're *begging.*"

"Man, they were passing the hat around *with photos of their children, explaining to people that their children needed medicine and operations back home.* They were *crying*, okay? That's begging. I was paying them ten thousand dollars for one weekend! Plus flights and hotel! But that would have been tolerable, if it wasn't for the tapes."

"Tapes?"

"They sold cassettes while they were *busking*."

"So the merchandise tent guys were mad that they were selling merch outside the tent, not payin' them their 15 percent cut of the action, eh?"

"Well, that would have been manageable."

"I guess they sold them for less than they would have cost in the merch tent, too, eh? Undercutting."

"*That* was not the problem."

"Well what, then?"

"The tapes were *blank*, man. They were selling them for ten bucks a pop to my audience, and when people took the tapes back to their Kitsilano homes, there was *nothing on them*. Just hiss. Never booking those guys again."

I guess I was supposed to take a cautionary lesson from that story. But me, that just made me love that band even more.

"Those Kitsilano people shoulda felt *honoured* to have bought blank tapes from the Changas. That's like getting shat on by a raven or something. It's good luck."

Then I'm pretty sure I might have changed tables and ranted at some sensitive Ontario folk kid about the evils of the Newfoundland band Great Big Sea, with their airbrushed harmonies, theme-park Irishness, and goddamned *Takkameany* guitars. Hate that band. They were on the main stage that night, smarmily romping about with their didley-dee smiley-smiley bullshit, fuelling me, motivating me in my crusades.

After that there's a vague memory of wandering up to the beautiful dancers from the Camerounian band as they shivered under thick blankets in the cool of the Canadian summer evening. I was just drunk enough to speak French at that point. They seemed pleased to finally meet someone who spoke it, in a country that had been, they felt, fraudulently pitched to them as bilingual. They complained about the bland quality of the food, especially the beef. I warned them not to say such things in English while in Alberta.

I know that Leslie Stark was kind of around the whole night, but I cagily slipped out of the vicinity any time she seemed to be headed my way. It wasn't hard, since everybody wanted to talk to her and she was mostly trying to get the attention of her assistant with the BlackBerry, to get an update on the attendance numbers for the night. I didn't spot Jimmy Kinnock, or more importantly, Richard Wren, his legendary string-puller.

I must have made it back to the hotel room, because that's where I woke up. Mykola was in the single bed next to mine, buried, snoring under the duvet.

THE MOTIVATOR

I WENT DOWN AND SCARED UP some breakfast from the coffee shop, returned to the room, and woke up Mykola by blowing bacon-tinged cigarette smoke in his face. I called Jenny and Manny to come over.

Manny started to manically jump around, climbing the furniture and talking a river of bullshit, like he does when he's nervous. Mykola ate everything on everybody's plates, and Jenny scowled.

"People are going to be expecting Athena to jam with Jimmy Kinnock. That's what they paid for. They're gonna tear us apart."

"They're not going to tear anybody apart. These are folkies. They don't tear. They whine, maybe. They harrumph. They mutter. They are not going to stone you, even if you blow it."

Manny launched into a soliloquy about "positive energy." I should have tolerated it, since he was trying to back me up, but I just couldn't bear it at 10:20 in the morning.

"Shut up. All right, listen: I don't want to hear any more about what the audience wants. Not only do these people have *no idea* what they want, but if they did, they'd probably be wrong to want it. *We* know what people need to hear. They need to hear *real fucking music*, not a *performance*, not fake, sanitized overly slick sentimental ritualized packaging of something that maybe once used to be real. That realness would still matter to them, if only they could hear it. If only they could hear the fundamental crazy emotions at the bottom of it. YOU PEOPLE CAN DO

THAT. And you're some of the very few here who can. As soon as you get up there and do what you know how to do, they'll forget all about what they thought they were there for. And just as importantly, Mister Richard Wren is going to forget about everything and want to be part of the feeling that you're going to create up there. Now fucking stop whining, and go out and fucking do what you were born to do."

There was some grumbling, but they picked up their instruments and started to move. I tell you, I am a supreme motivator of artists.

As we marched across the park toward the stage, I kept my sharpshooter eyes systematically scanning the flow and counterflow of sunburned crowd for any sign of Leslie Stark's explosion of black curly hair, but I guess she was off dealing with some emergency. There'd been a rumour the night before that some famous American roots singer-songwriter lady had arrived fresh from a divorce and was insisting on playing none of her hits, instead wanting to "try out" all-new songs that she'd written over the past several grief-stricken days. To add to the effect, the Star was planning on doing all her appearances for the weekend in a Muslim Burqua made out of the American flag. If I was her manager, I would have backed her 100 percent. And it was also good luck for us, keeping Leslie busy.

Manny whistled and sang, capering about, waving to all and sundry. Jenny was doing some kind of breathing exercise as she walked. Mykola was clutching a cheeseburger he'd managed to grab on the way over. He stared at the grass as he forced himself forward, occasionally bumping into the odd hippy or young vegan anarchist and splattering beefy relish on them.

"Watch yer step, Mykola. I need to deliver you to the stage without anything broken."

"It's just … so nervous. Saw Jimmy Kinnock when I was just a kid. This one Woody Guthrie song he played, 'Deportees,' it changed my life."

"You're *still* a kid. And for God's sake, don't tell *him* that. He's probably sick to death of having that conversation. Okay? All right?"

"Yeah, okay."

"You're gonna be fine." I waved my hands at him, ceremoniously. "I'm putting an Invisible Success Force-Field around you. Okay?"

"Okay."

Poor bastard has terrible stage fright, right up until the moment that he actually gets on stage. Then he's instantly more comfortable than he is in the whole rest of his life.

We reached Stage Five, one of the workshop stages.

"Hey, Cam." Oh, shit. Sandy Mackenzie.

"Sandy! Good to see you, man."

"Oh, yeah?"

"Hey, you've got a volunteer shirt on. You working on this stage?"

"I'm the stage manager. 'Cause I'm a store manager now in real life, instead of a wastrel."

"Hunh." What the hell do you say to something like that?

"These your current victims, here?"

"You bet."

"Hey Sandy!" chirped Manny.

"Hey Manny. You really still work with Scam-bull, do ya?"

"Seems like it. Too dumb to quit. Ha-ha."

"Maybe I should let these younger people in on a few things about working with you, Cam."

"Yeah, maybe you should. After. In the meantime, I think the workshop's starting in, like, seven minutes."

"Jeez, Cam, that's not like you to *under*estimate how little time there is to get something done. So. Where's Athena Amarok?"

"She's not here. New plan: these guys will just play their own stuff in the slot where Athena would have played."

Sandy pursed his lips. "Yeah? So where is she, though?"

"I got a message this morning saying her floatplane was delayed and she missed her connecting flight in Whitehorse. Has to wait for the next one. Now can we get rolling on the setup, here?"

"Just for the record, just so's you know, *buddy*, I know you're lying right now."

I decided to just say nothing and stare at him blankly, to see if he really wanted to get into all of our past bullshit right now and delay the show.

There was a pause.

"Okay, well, you guys better tell me your mic specs, then after the show, Cam, maybe you and I can have a little talk about the final report for the travel grants on that Europe tour you screwed us on five years ago."

"Sure thing, Sandy. Okay, let's get this thing rolling."

THE CIRCUMSTANCES IN WHICH HE QUIT THE BAND

MACKENZIE DOESN'T DRINK ANYMORE. He manages a health-food store in Calgary now. But when he did, he was heroic about it. Besides the sheer legendary scale of his drinking, I guess the main difference between his consumption and mine was that he didn't ever do it for fun. He never got to that moment of cheerful *bonhomie* where everybody links arms and sings "Galway Bay." He was serious about drinking, like the Finns, not talking at all for long periods while he addressed himself to the bottle.

Sandy was the nominal "leader" of that hardcore punk band I mentioned before. We'd been on a hell of a roll of good luck up until when his sister drank a bunch of pills and checked out of her confused, fucked-up life. I could tell at the funeral that Sandy was in no shape to go out on the tour I'd planned out. I cancelled everything and bought a case of Southern Comfort with the advances. Sandy and I spent the next three months in the basement of his mom's house, playing Ping-Pong and shooting the nasty, mouthwashy liquor. Karyn had been a big fan of her brother's music, helped out at the shows, and was a leading light in the local hardcore scene in general. Somehow it was immediately apparent that hardcore was the last thing we wanted to hear during that period. It was too positive to fit our mood.

We found ourselves listening to his mom's old Gordon Lightfoot, Ian and Sylvia, and Johnny Cash records a lot. This was the stuff we'd always said we hated, and somehow it was giving us more deep comfort than anything else except the booze and the Ping-Pong. Ping-Pong is a beacon of hope in a troubled world. I guess we were sort of understanding that when shit goes truly bad, you wind up resetting to your roots or something. "*I never got over those blue eyes ...*"

When he started to pick up the guitar again, it just seemed natural to start playing those songs, and when he started writing again, it was country songs, with some of that punk sneer, that came out. I had him revive a couple of his old hardcore songs, and it turned out that after all they were country songs, too, if you played them right. We just hadn't known it.

I helped him assemble a band, with some of the same players as before. People started calling it Cowpunk. People said it was the coming thing. I didn't care about that. It just felt more subversive, somehow, to fuck with the kind of music that regular people actually liked.

I've found a lot of Truly Greats, with my uncanny, laser-like talent for spotting talent. Some of them have come closer to the Brass Ring of Success than others. Sandy and his band were Truly Great, and I came close to getting them the Brass Ring. But the two big problems that usually come with the Truly Greats are that they tend to be Ahead of Their Time, and Their Own Worst Enemy. Sandy's group were definitely Ahead of Their Time. And I'll tell you, near the end of the band, Sandy was like an eight-division army of Worst Enemies for himself, with air support.

When we used to play places like, say, Red Deer, where the band had a good following — so we had what you call an "open bar" situation — he'd walk in, and before load-in (being a lead singer, he rarely helped with load-in anyway) he'd order a row of eight shots of Jägermeister. As the bartender lined 'em up for him,

Mackenzie would pull out the big pink bottle of Pepto-Bismol that I made sure he kept with him at all times.

He was only twenty-seven by then, but he'd already hurt his stomach lining so bad with hard liquor that in order to drink at all, he needed to take a big swig of the chalky-minty-sweet antacid medicine as a prophylactic measure. When I first started seeing him double over in agony, clutching his belly before the set, I knew just what to do, having seen my dear old dad dealing with the very same issues when I was just a nipper. I went right to the twenty-four-hour Shoppers Drug Mart to get what was needed for Sandy's condition.

Through the rumour factory of the Canadian independent music scene, which runs in three contiguous eight-hour shifts, I've heard some people call me an "enabler" of Sandy's drinking. Some of those people include Sandy, just to tell you how ungrateful these yowling string-pluckers can be. But I was his Manager. What is the word *manage*, really, if it's not essentially a synonym for *enable*, I ask you? And if I sometimes felt that I had to Manage, in a participatory manner, some of Sandy's epic eight-month drinking bouts, all I can say is, how far are *you* willing to go to keep a Truly Great musical outfit running? I go to the limit, my friend. Every goddamn time.

Since I was essentially the glue that held them together for those last couple of years, on the never-ending tour in support of their final album, *Burning the Furniture to Keep Warm*; since I was the Rock on which the operation was founded, it naturally falls to me now to tell the actual, True version of how Judge Brighton came to quit the band. And frankly, once he was gone, that was it.

THERE IS NOWHERE AND NOTHING between Thunder Bay and Winnipeg. It's just endless driving over flat rock, forever. I try to explain it to Europeans as the distance between Amsterdam and Kazakhstan, but they never believe me. Look it up, it's true.

Sandy's strategy for dealing with the mind-numbing melancholy horror of the boredom of the unending Canadian plains was to numb his mind even further, aiming for unconsciousness for the whole trip. That turned the journey into a kind of teleportation, like on *Star Trek*, he used to say. Sandy loved *Star Trek*. One time, he closed his eyes on the outskirts of Thunder Bay and didn't open them till we got to Vegreville, Alberta, 3,000 kilometres away. Vegreville has the World's Biggest Easter Egg. When the van stopped to refuel in front of this massive Ukrainian monstrosity, I had to get somebody to wake him up to get more gas money out of him. The first thing he said, digging in to his wallet, was, "This shit is got to stop." Not sure what he was going for, there. Then he dragged himself out of the van, stretched audibly, saw the giant painted egg, and observed, "Hey, we got one of those things in Alberta — in Vegreville." That kind of oblivion was his ideal.

Needless to say, this shirking of any driving duties, the moaning, the implied duty of the rest of the group (usually me) to nudge him now and then to make sure he wasn't dead, and the smell when he invariably pissed himself and lay that way for days afterward, that all exacerbated the effect of the various irritating aspects of his personality in those days. Other fun habits he'd developed included the sartorial decision to wear whatever outfit he'd last got laid in, *ad nauseum*, and a recent tendency to threaten hitherto-friendly journalists with a punch in the chops if they mentioned the word "cowpunk" in his presence. "Music ain't about labels, man." Oh, yeah, and that was the tour where we opened for this Big-in-Canada band called Blue Rodeo, in Peterborough, and he called their singer Jim Cuddy a "Pretty Boy Cocksucker" and then dropped to his knees and, staying with the cock-sucking theme, offered to suck *his* cock and swallow if Cuddy would just promise not to play their simpering love-ballad hit song "Try" that night.

So things were going great.

Judge Brighton, in particular, was on edge about the situation.

Judge was the youngest in the band, and Sandy had been his idol for years, long before he actually became a member. He was only allowed to join the outfit at first because the kid wouldn't stop following Sandy around anyway, and in the beginning they just made him sell T-shirts, but then it turned out he could tune guitars, which was handy, and then it turned out he could play keyboards, and then it turned out he could play lead guitar, too, then it turned out he was actually the best musician in the band.

Judge was a brainy kid. His dad was a professor. The boy read Kierkegaard and listened to Gang of Four. When he first heard Sandy's band, he'd been a teenage volunteer at the local university radio station, and they came in to play live on the air. Kid was amazed. Changed his life.

With Sandy, Judge made that classic error of mistaking a laconic guy for a guy with a lot of amazing shit on his mind that he didn't deem you worthy of talking to you about. If you get seduced into trying to "get to the bottom" of a guy like that, you might be a little bit pissed off at what you find in the end.

To be fair, Sandy was a hell of a songwriter. He wrote about our obscure pointless little lives in a boring backwater of a boring country as if we were all dramatic heroes of great consequence and romance, and it was convincing. Shit, the spell was so effective, when I look back on it now, we were all living in a Sandy Mackenzie song for about seven years there. But as a person, at the time, he was really just a drunk, selfish, morose, skinny little fuck whose inner life was a narrow universe of self-destructive self-mythology. Judge had a calling to be a musician for life, and was developing into a genius songwriter himself, not that Sandy would admit it, and over a period of about two years, his disillusion with Sandy and Sandy's shenanigans had come pretty close to completing itself. He was *just about there* ...

Also, Judge was doing a lot of speed then. That might have accounted for some of the edginess, too, I guess.

SO SANDY WAS PURSUING HIS teleportation concept when he downed several painkillers, a few Tums, and a mickey of Southern Comfort and wedged himself down in the back, with the equipment, as we pulled out of the Tim Hortons parking lot, still with the irreversibly polluted Lake Superior in view.

I guess his tolerance for depressants had gone up since the last trip, because we'd only been driving for about seven hours when we heard a banging from the back. The threatening sound of glass on metal. *Clank! Clank!*

Sandy poked his head up from behind the seats, goggle-eyed.

"Ey! S'no mre SouthrnCmfrt! Who the fuck drank it?"

"You did, you idiot!"

"Rmph."

He crumpled back down.

This repeated itself a couple more times, but then somewhere around Brandon, Manitoba, the clanking started up again, but this time it was *Clank! Clank! … Smash!*

Sandy was in a rage, demanding to know who the fuck kind of bastard would steal a man's liquor? What kind of fuck?

He threw the broken mickey forward. It hit Jeanine the backup singer keyboard player in the side of the head, making her bleed. Being a true tough Albertan girl, she waved it off, saying it was nothing. But for Judge Brighton, crashing on the speed, looking at the blood, it was a fuse-lighter. Before I could react, he picked up the bloody, headless bottle and stared at it, growling in a keening, animalistic kind of way.

He hurled himself at Sandy like a stone age cruise missile, screaming, "I'll fucking KILL you!" Actually landed with his hands clasped right around Sandy's throat. Sandy's body having no more heft or balance than a freestanding pool cue, they both continued in the direction of Judge's momentum, into the equipment area at the very back, into the door, slamming it open.

I'm not embarrassed to say that I've always had a lightning-quick sense for danger — I'm not bragging, it's just a fact — and my danger sense told me that the bass player was just about to stand on the brakes. That same sense also told me that a sudden deceleration would have been exactly the wrong thing to do. With split-second alacrity, I shouted to the driver — "Maintain this speed exactly! I'll deal with this!"

Naturally, even I had no idea whatsoever how I was going to deal with it as I scrambled over the seats.

When I reached the situation, I saw the kid holding Sandy's throat, with Sandy's head and shoulders hiked out over Canada Highway Number 1, as it rolled by under him at 140 kilometres an hour.

"I'll KILL you! I'll KILL you!" was Brighton's key theme.

"No! No! Hey!" was about the best I could do. I worried that if I grabbed for something or somebody, it would all go awry and I'd wind up having to walk back several miles, collecting pieces of both of them with one of those garbage pokers, putting them in a sack for later cremation.

But Sandy was calm, just lying there as the prairie and the asphalt and his own gruesome demise whizzed by, inches away.

"Gimme one reason why I shouldn't! You waste everything you touch!" Judge screamed.

"Don't do it, Judge." said Sandy, in a preternaturally urbane, dreamy way.

"Gimme one good reason!" Even at this moment of crisis, it was funny in a way to hear him lapsing into action-movie dialogue — the boy had such a fastidious horror of cliché most of the time.

"Gimme one good reason!"

I could smell the oily exhaust of the Ford Econoline farting up from the tailpipe, mixing with the puke-and-Drum-Tobacco scent of Sandy's leather jacket, Brighton's musty lumberjack shirt, and a faint note of wet potato — Brandon, Manitoba, used to be the clearing house for McDonald's french fries for all of North America. I remember it so clearly.

Sandy looked his former acolyte in the eyes, and spoke slowly. "If you do, my troubles'll be over, but *your* life'll be ruined. Don't ruin your life for me, man. I'm not worth it."

Judge paused. Exhaled. And hauled him back into the van.

"You're right. I quit."

Sandy soldiered on for another year after that, but there was no question that right then at that moment, that was it for that band.

NOW THE WORKSHOP ITSELF

Naturally, it went just exactly as great as I always knew it would. You may not be familiar with the idea of a "workshop" in a Canadian folk festival. The most important thing to understand about it is that it's not a workshop. No work gets done, and nobody learns anything. What you do, you get three to five different acts up on one stage — people who often don't know each other, who play different styles of music, who might not even like each other. Each act takes a turn playing a song. The act that's playing might or might not invite the other acts to play along, and those other acts might or might not choose to accept that invitation to play along.

The result can be absolute cacophony and chaos. When a Pakistani circus brass band jams along with the Scottish piper and the Mexican cowboy outfit, you can wind up with the aural equivalent of a haggis doused with sag paneer wrapped in a taco.

But the secret of the workshop format is, when the Pakistani haggis taco surprises everybody and tastes good, then the audience feels like it's been witness to a bloody miracle, which they have. It's the quotidian miracle of what music can do for you, so fucking help me.

In this workshop, we had my crew of reprobates, plus the legendary British punk folk star, Jimmy Kinnock, the one managed by Richard Wren, in case I forgot to remind you enough. Also, we had a pretty half-Maori girl from New Zealand who sang trad and original material with some kind of loop pedal gimmick that allowed her to harmonize with herself. Then for added spice, we had this guy, I can't remember his name; he was ostensibly a Norwegian Sami guy, who engaged in this traditional kind of singing/toasting vocalizing thing called Joiking. But he didn't look Sami to me — he was as pale and aboriginal-looking as Truman Capote. Anyway, he did his Joiking overtop of the standard looped warmed-over nineties hip-hop beats, "played" on a laptop by some anonymous dude with fashionable spectacles.

My personal favourite moment was in the Joiker's main song. He and his buddy with the laptop were going for it, super full-on (in their own minds, anyway), raising the dynamic tension (actually just getting louder and louder), and then the Joiker would point to somebody with his traditional sceptre thingy, indicating that it was time for them to take their solo. Manny did his crazy animal-sound thing to much applause, and the "Sami" came over and gave him a big, emotional hug, as the beat went on. Then he looked over at Jimmy Kinnock, who kind of shrugged and looked at the guy, a look which very efficiently conveyed the message: "I have no idea what you think I could do here, mate, because I'm just a folk singer, I sing folk songs, and I have nothing to contribute to your weird pseudo-aboriginal jam." So the Joiker pretended he hadn't even looked over at him in the first place, and cast his theatrically intense gaze at the pretty New Zealand half-Maori girl.

She was more than ready to pick up the baton, and began this kind of amorphous singing that oddly reminded me a bit of Athena, without the balls. I've seen Athena eat raw seal heart with relish, her face all bloody. This girl sounded vegan.

I think her thing was kind of based on *some* kind of Maori traditional thing, but there was a cheesy Whitney Houston/ Mariah Carey kind of aspect to it, too, and she kept raising her voice in the manner of a suburban housewife faking an orgasm, which I guess was a turn-on for *some* people, because when she was done her solo, as the backing track continued, the Joiker dude came over to *her* and gave her a bit more than Manny's comradely bear hug. He started with a nice, friendly embrace, but once he had her pinned, as the cheesy beats and bass thumped away, he sucked onto her face and literally stuck his tongue right down her throat, causing her to kind of freeze in a horribly uncomfortable way, although Buddy didn't seem to notice or mind. He went at her for a good minute before he pulled out and then pointed his sceptre thingy at Jenny Reid, in a kind of "you're next" kind of way.

Jenny nodded over at Manny, who stopped his playing to give her space, and she went into a decent little slapping bass solo. The bass jocks in the crowd went wild, drowned out by all the girls, and she just smouldered out at them, not looking at Joikey at all.

But when the solo came to an end and the drums kicked back in, Joikey started dancing over toward her, clearly looking for some more lovin'. Jenny deftly picked up a drum stick from the kit nearby and glowered at him. She made a gesture with the drumstick that was meaningfully anatomical, and he wisely decided to boogie backwards, toward his own spot.

All that's beside the point of the total triumph of the workshop, which was all about the artists *I* brought to the table. Jenny played a song that was inarguably obscene, in which she, as a lesbian, got away with talking about the object of her desire, essentially, as a piece of meat. No male folksinger would ever even contemplate singing a song like that, and rightly so, because he'd be run out of town on a rail. But with Jenny singing it, she not only had the (sizable) lady-loving lady contingent in the audience singing along, but all the straight men in the crowd grabbed hold of this opportunity to sing nasty lyrics about tits in public, all in the spirit of supporting a marginalized voice of gay pride, of course. Naturally, Mister Jimmy chortled along in his best cockney barker voice. There wasn't a dry seat in the house.

Mykola was a big fan of Jimmy Kinnock and knew half his songs, so he did a very worthy job of plunking along on his kobza and singing backups. When it was his turn to play his own tune, he played a funny little love song he'd written on the way up, and in the manner of these things, I noticed many of the girls in the audience looking at him just slightly *differently*, if you know what I mean.

Which is all as much as to say that by the time the hour and a half was over, everybody had completely forgotten that Athena's name was on the list of performers. Several hundred people had discovered music they'd never known existed, and many rushed up to the back of the tent-stage to meet their new favourite artists.

One of them, I recognized immediately, was the stately, genial, white-haired presence of Mr. Richard Wren himself.

He ambled up to the barrier line and ducked under, calling out, "Right ho, Jimbo!" as he moved. Kinnock waved to him, but then Wren made a beeline for Mykola and Jenny, who were packing up their instruments. He had a big smile on his face, his right hand extended to shake.

"Bloody great! Bloody great, you two!"

I strode toward the situation, my own right hand extended for interception.

"Cam Ouiniette, Mister Wren. I'm these geniuses' manager."

"Well, I tell you that was bloody great. The real stuff, there. Don't see it that much these days, you know."

"See!" I whapped Jenny on the back and tousled Mykola's hair. "I told you you had the goods. Listen, Mr. Wren, I'm hoping we can have a chat about these two."

"Absolutely!"

"Ah, there you are, Cam." There was Sandy, of course. And he had his awful wife with him.

"You've got some explaining to do, mister. We've had some letters from Revenue Canada demanding income tax on money that Sandy never even made!"

"Listen, Sharon, can I talk to you guys later about this?"

Wren, as a top-flight manager, clearly recognized the awkward situation I was in. I once read in a rock tell-all book about a roadie taking a broken light bulb to Wren's throat in order to get paid his wage for a tour. He began to back away.

"Listen, yeah, why don't we chat later tonight. See you at the After-Party, I understand Buckwheat Zydeco's playing, yeah?"

"Yeah, sure. I'll see you there."

Sharon Mackenzie took my arm. "You come with us. We have some things to discuss."

COME ALL YE BOLD CANADIANS

AFTER I HAD BLAGUED AND BULLSHITTED Sandy and his wife for a while with various half-truths, red herrings. and false promises, and they had yelled at me, and I had yelled at them, they finally had to let me go, since Sandy, who is still quite slight of build and has replaced booze with weed, was not going to hit me, after all.

I was feeling pretty low at that point. Then I just happened to glance down at the cellphone. Three missed calls from a Vancouver number. I didn't want to recognize it, but there was no mistaking that number. It was of course the payphone on Commercial Drive, just up the hill from our apartment on East Fourth. I didn't really want to know, but in case it was a medical emergency with Maevey, I needed to just quickly check it.

So yes, I did hear your message, my Love, telling me that the phone had been cut off at home, and I heard your sadness and anger in your voice when you said, "You *said* that you'd *paid* it, but the phone company says that we owe *five hundred and forty-five dollars,* and I *need* the phone in order to register for my university courses in the fall, and could you *please call me?*"

Yes, okay, I did get the following two messages, where the anger boiled off, leaving thick despair. My thinking was, *I've got something absolutely brilliant on the go. I have to stay absolutely focused on the mission at hand, so that I can return as the conquering hero, with cash and a major management deal in hand.* Yes, I did spend the phone money on the rental van to get us to the festival, because I'd spent the travel money on the cellphone bill and part of my tab at Café Vasco da Gama, because I'd spent the pay I got from the last Canada Council for the Arts grant on a plane ticket to Nunavut, et cetera., backwards in a never-ending chain of spinning plates of barely serviced debts and expenses. But I was certain, given my abilities, and the talent I work with, thanks to my amazing ear for musical genius, I was certain that I would bring back such an amazing carload of magic beans that all would be forgiven. It's an old saying, but still powerful as ever as a rule for living: It's easier to ask for forgiveness than permission.

I'm sorry, I'm so sorry my Love. I should have called you. But can't anyone see why it seemed wrong to do so at the time? I had to Stay On Target, and to do that, I had to get my head together.

I WAS SHAKEN, SHAKEN BY the sound of your voice falling slowly, unglamourously out of love with me. So at that moment, I just found myself unable to cope in the complex hand-to-hand social battlefield of the backstage beer garden, where managers, agents, bookers for festivals, and lastly, musicians and the people they are hoping to sleep with, congregate in a drunken, milling hornet's nest. I needed hard liquor, and I needed proper music. I gripped the Nalgene bottle full of Scotch in my bag and marched out to hear Paddy McGraw play the main stage.

Not too close to the stage, just back a bit, and to stage left, where I could see the man do his thing without worrying about people jockeying around me for a better view. Or so I thought.

Paddy McGraw, eighty-three years old, the mentor for all the young Cape Breton fiddlers who came down to Toronto out of Nova Scotia and got their hair up in a gelled quiff and laid their birthright down on top of generic nineties hip-hop beats that Chuck D wouldn't have bothered comment on as he tossed them out the studio window, Paddy McGraw, still better than them all, still innovating and messing around with the tradition in ways that few would understand, but some could feel.

Watch those fingers if you like, for their uncanny speed, even in their ninth decade, see the fingers fly, but listen, *listen* to what he's doing. He's got ahold of the tune so it's talking about the fire of his youth, and the regrets of his middle age, and the return to the home note is a coming-to-terms with it all in old age that never entirely resolves, an intentional dissonance filled with awe at the things a man can see and do in one lifetime and still never truly understand the world and its terrible wonder, a dissonance that announces that this musician hasn't finished his story, and just maybe if there's any pretty ladies out there interested, this old boy still has a few surprises up his kilt, and the hustle just might still be on, no quarter given.

This is a tune that every student of Celtic fiddle from St. John's, Newfoundland, to Galway to Newcastle-Upon-Tyne to Osaka, Japan, is taught in their first year, a tune that was played a hundred thousand times by travelling minstrels under a thousand different names, the way you do when you're in that life: "Oh, your Excellency, your hospitality has been so perfect and so kind, I've been inspired to write a piece of music for you, and with your permission I'd like to name it for you, the Duke of Bunbury's Reel" or whatever the name of your patron that night might be ...

"Excuse me!"

I turned. A late-middle-aged, bearded, pot-bellied man in yet another Genuine First Nations sweater, with his wife, who resembled him.

"Excuse me! We're trying to enjoy the music."

"Well, there's no reason why you shouldn't enjoy it, it just takes a leap of imagination and a bit of human feeling."

You see, I know how to deal with Canadians.

WE WERE NOT TRAPPED, PART II

"WE DON'T HAVE A DOG IN THIS FIGHT," said Andy McKay, tapping his Cross pen on his blue, pinstriped, be-suited knee. From behind his desk, Queen Elizabeth II and her bland, meaningless smile looked on from the wall.

"Actually, Andy, I think we have several dogs in this fight. There's Canadians mixed up in every side of this bloody circus. I hear that the Croatian defence minister used to run a pizza joint in Brantford, Ontario."

"Well, fine, Mr. Ouiniette. But you get involved in these things at your own risk. The Yugoslavian conflict is the result of centuries of frankly barbaric ethnic hatred — it goes back to the Stone Age, practically. We can't begin to understand it, and, very frankly, we don't care to, either. We can get your Canadians out on the next flight, but we can't do anything about your … friends. That is not within the bounds of our power. We're just here to maintain the ceasefire. Peacekeeping. That's what we do. We don't just take twenty random foreign people, put them in a Sea King, and fly them to Canada."

"These people aren't random. By giving us sanctuary, they saved our lives, and also, as far as I can see, there's no fucking peace to keep here. These people are the cream of Sarajevo avant garde artistic expression." I left out the part about them all being members of the Sarajevo Aleister Crowley Reading Group, and the part about them being currently holed up at the mansion of a notorious Albanian gangster. "Each one of them has more culture in a single eyelash than the entire city of Kingston." That part was true. "Where are you from, Andy?"

"P.E.I., originally. St. Andrews."

"Well, there you go, they could form an artistic colony on Prince Edward Island, stage Situationist Happenings for the Japanese tourists. You'd have to agree, as a Prince Edward Islander, it'd make a nice change from all the horrific, soul-killing Anne of Green Gables garbage. My point is, if you don't get them out, they're gonna be fucking murdered."

"That's a little overdramatic, don't you think?"

"No, I think *you're* being typically, Canadianly *underdramatic*. What is it with Canadians and their psychotic need to *downplay* everything serious, extraordinary, *crazy*. 'Nothin' to see here, folks, move along.' I *know* that by not giving them some sort of asylum, I *know*, and you know too, that they're gonna get *fucked*. It's a mixed-ethnic group. Serbs married to Croats, Croats married to Macedonians, Muslims." I left out the ones that were in four- or five-way open relationships. "If the Yugo bastard Serb army don't get 'em, the fucking Croat Nazis will."

"Well, as I said, there's nothing we can do about that. We'll get you and your Canadian musicians out, but we can't help the others. We just can't. I don't even have the authority to do anything."

From the fact that he was making excuses now, I could see he was almost imperceptibly cracking. "There's a crack in everything," I heard an old man say once.

"Do you know who Raoul Wallenberg was, Andrew?"

"Yes, I know."

"He was a Swedish diplomat who smuggled thousands of Jews outta Nazi territory, without the permission of his government."

"I said 'yes, I know,' already, okay?"

"He saved thousands of lives, Andy."

"I said 'I know!'"

"He was a Hero."

"He also wound up dead."

"We all wind up dead, Andy. But who among us, *who among us* does anything *extraordinary, honourable, noble* with their lives?"

"You think I'm really that easy to play, my friend?"

"I'm not trying to play you, man. I'm just looking for a solution, here. Okay, look: here's all I need from you: ten cartons of smokes and a case of vodka from the PX. — put down that there was a diplomatic party with the Chinese consulate or something — and an official letter from the Canadian government, in English, denying my people their application for aid in leaving the country."

"Denying it?"

"Yeah. Not a scrap of evidence will exist that says you helped. You keep a copy, so your ass is covered. Just give me 5 minutes in the PX."

"What are you going to do?"

"Nothing bad. Help me out that much, willya, Raoul?"

COME ALL YE BOLD
CANADIANS CONTINUED

SORRY, I WAS IN THE MIDDLE of telling you about Paddy McGraw's killer performance that those middle-aged Canadian folkies were trying to interrupt, when I interrupted myself. I've got to try harder to stay with the story.

Anyway, the man in the Genuine Indian Handmade sweater says, "You're *standing* in the sitting area."

"Alright, I'll siddown." I plunked myself to the ground.

"You can't sit here, we got here at 9 a.m. to put our blanket down here."

Oh, there it was. The twilight slowly revealed the tartan blanket, the plastic cooler, the stupid, stupid little no-leg chairs with the festival logo on them. Christ.

"Well, I'm either going to sit here or stand here. This is my man Paddy McGraw and I'm not going to miss him."

"Well, this is our spot."

I turned to him and growled. "So go call the cops. You'll miss the greatest fiddler alive for the sake of your own pettiness."

The man and wife mounted an assault on my presence in the usual Canadian way. A low-level, muttering dialogue on the subject of how *some* people think that the whole world was made for them and the rules don't apply to them and was that alcohol they smelled because you're not allowed to drink alcohol on the festival grounds outside the beer tent and *some* people were going to get thrown out on their ear.

In a perfect answer to a prayer I didn't even know I'd specifically uttered, Paddy finished his reel, lowered his fiddle, and launched into a bizarre, furious, *a cappella* shouting rendition of the old folk song "Come All Ye Bold Canadians," a battle hymn from the War of 1812, forgotten for decades everywhere but the little outposts of Cape Breton:

> *Come All Ye Bold Canadians and gird your trusty might!*
> *Let's make the American libertines regret they picked a fight!*
> *For Order and Good Government, we'll fight for what is right!*
> *Come All Ye Bold Canadians and gird your trusty might!*

> *The perfidious rebels snuck across our border by the score,*
> *They raped the nuns on tables, threw the babies to the floor.*
> *(what cads!)*
> *But Invincible General Brock was ready when he heard the call,*
> *He drove them back and now he'll chase them over hedge and wall.*

> *So Come All Ye Bold Canadians and gird your trusty might!*
> *Let's make the American libertines regret they picked a fight!*
> *For Order and Good Government, we'll fight for what is right!*
> *Come All Ye Bold Canadians and gird your trusty might!*

*Around the world Canadians are feared as soldiers
bold.
Loyal and obedient, we'll kill and die when told.
(Yes, sir!)
Liberty is not for me, I know my rightful place:
Upon my knees before Our King whom God
enthron'd with Grace.*

*Come All Ye Bold Canadians and gird your trusty
might!
Let's make the American libertines regret they picked
a fight!
For Order and Good Government, we'll fight for
what is right!
Come All Ye Bold Canadians and gird your trusty
might!*

And I was roaring along with the chorus, and soon most of my
neighbours were, too, till we came to what I knew (but they didn't)
was coming, the horrifying final verse:

*No matter where they run and hide, we'll chase
them down like dogs.
We'll burn the hated White House down with kero-
sene and logs.
A Godless slave of Liberty deserves just what he gets,
Their livestock, wives, and unborn brats will feel
our bayonets!*

I collapsed in a drunken shattering uproar of my worst barroom
laughter, spluttering saliva in a generous radius with each guffaw.

I went backstage, waiting for McGraw to be helped down the
steps by a young lady volunteer. I told myself that I just had to
shake this man's hand, because he is the Real Thing, but also of

course I was leaving while the getting was good, slipping into the dark, away from Mr. and Mrs. Short Chair, and marching purposefully past the backstage security sentry, waving my all-access pass.

The young blond volunteer was laudably conscientious in her efforts to get the old feller to solid ground, letting him lean way into her when he almost missed the second to last step. "Oops-a-daisy."

"Thank you so much, my dear," he said, with a kindly twinkle of his eye. "That last step was a doozy."

"My pleasure, Mr. McGraw. Great set tonight! I love your music."

"Well thank you, thank you."

I politely drew closer to this legendary figure, as the young volunteer gamboled away toward her next assignment. I suppose there's just something about my appearance or demeanor that makes people comfortable enough to share what's on their mind, because as I approached him, he looked me in the eye, grinned a crinkly grin, motioned with his head toward the departing young lady and said, "Like to get *that* greased up on all fours on the hotel room carpet, eh?"

SUPERSONIC GRIFTERS

THERE'S A POND BEHIND A HILL in the park outside the gates. It's surrounded by a copse of pine trees. I was just gonna find myself a little silence, maybe. Get my head together before the big push to seduce Wren at the After-Party at the hotel.

But when I was rounding the hill, I heard talking and other noises. Giggling. Snuffling.

"Hey! What are you punks doin' behind that tree, this is the Caaal-gary police!" I shouted in my most Authoritarian voice.

"Jesus, fuck! DD! Quick!"

I jumped out in front of them, tongue out, hair flying, fingers waggling. "Boo! Gabbadoo!"

"Fuck! It's you! You fucking gave me a heart attack," exhaled the banjo player, the tall, tattooed guy who'd been singing outside the gates.

"We almost threw away the drugs!" That was the little fiddler, not accusative, just cheerful that the drugs had been saved.

They were gathered round a Crass seven-inch 45 record cover, using it as a flat surface on the banjo's hard case to snort something white.

The mother guitar player girl came from behind a tree, where I could see the baby sleeping in a car seat and the skinny handsome guitar kid in the top hat zipping up his pants, looking spent. "Oh look, it's Mister Important!"

"That's a great Crass single. *Pictures of Starving Children Sell Records*. Always loved the cover."

"Yeah, wull, it's a good single for doing coke off of."

"So you're spending the day's take on drugs, eh?"

"Only half of it. We're saving the other half. *Right* guys?" said the Young Mother.

"Ye-es, Amy." They sing-songed, like dutiful children.

"They've been running on trucker's speed for the last ten days, so I thought they deserved something a bit nicer, since we did so well out there."

"Calgary's an amazing coke town," observed the pretty, tough, gutbucket-player girl. The reluctant, rueful tone with which she delivered this remark implied that she of course despised Calgary, but nevertheless, you had to respect the quality of its blow.

"It's all those oil dudes. They got more money than they know what to do with. And they demand the best," said the tattooed banjo player. "That's the Alberta Advantage," he intoned in a deep TV announcer voice. Then he sucked up a line.

"Where are you guys staying?"

"Mostly in the van. I try to get them to take a hotel room once a week, to try to make them shower."

The fiddler smelled her own armpit with relish. "Mmmmmm. I stiiiiiiink."

"Where you parked? Denny's?"

"How'd you know?"

"But of course. So what's it like in there? Any good music going on?" asked the Mother.

"I wanna see Paddy McGraw," said the fiddler.

"Fuck, that fucking dinosaur?" was the pretty gutbucket girl's response.

"He's good," was all the fiddler said to defend her opinion.

I played my Mister Important card. "I just met him."

"No way!"

"Uh-hunh."

"Did you get a look at what kind of bow he was using?"

"Uh, no. But you're right. He's good."

She took up a big, long line. "Woop!"

I turned to the Mother. "So you and your child ride along with these miscreants? Aren't you afraid for his welfare?"

"We have very strict rules."

The band recited: "No drinking whiskey while driving."

"No eating the baby's food."

There was a pause.

"Those are all the rules, eh?"

"Yep. And they're strictly enforced."

"Well, I don't know if most people would consider those the only rules required for raising a Stable, Secure Child."

"I need the music to live. So the child can suck it if he doesn't like it."

"Hunh. You said suck it. About a baby." The big tattooed banjoist sniggered.

"Hey, kids, why don't you offer Mister Important some of your nice cocaine? Then maybe he'll like us more and want to help our 'musical career.'" It was clear that although this Amy girl was about the same age as the others, having a baby to lug around had thrown her into the default role of the Responsible One. She was trying to cloak her anxiety about it in an Ironic Grown-up Voice. Straining to stop Motherhood from robbing her of her Cool.

"You want some coke, Mister Important?" offered the handsome skinny fellow, with a close, eyeball-to-eyeball stare. He was challenging me. Or he thought he was.

"Don't mind if I do." As I hoovered it up, I wondered if Richard Wren would be willing to go this far to scout new talent. Maybe at one time, in the Psychedelic Era. Now? Please. This here was part of what I could bring to the table in a co-management arrangement.

"Offer him some of the screech, too."

"Oh, do we have to?"

"Yes, you do. Real Newfoundland screech? Where'd you get that?"

"Newfoundland. We were just there."

"Wow. You must have a better van than I thought you'd have."

"It's pretty good. Seventies Econoline. Don't need a computer to spot what's broken. Easy to get parts." This was the little fiddler.

"You repair it yourself?

"DD says she was born with a crescent wrench in her back pocket. I have no idea what that means."

"Bet you'd like to find out what I mean."

"Shut up. Goofball."

"How long have you horrid people been out on the road?"

"Five months. We went down to Santa Cruz, across to New Orleans, up through Maine to the Maritimes, took the ferry to Cornerbrook."

"We almost hit a moose this one time on the drive to St. John's."

"Three times! Three meese!"

I turned to the fiddle player. "Where the Hell you learn to play like that, son?"

"Port Alberni, British Columbia."

"The fuck you say."

"The fuck I *do* say. *Fuck.* I said it."

"I'll be damned."

"Me, too, if you ask my German mother."

"Port Alberni. Your dad a fisherman, or a mill worker?"

"My dad's a drunk." She took a no-nonsense pull on the screech and passed it to me.

"Fair enough." I raised the bottle to that and we locked eyes, for a moment, to signify our connection as drunk children of serious drunks. "My old man got hurt by a cow, once. Lost a lot of blood. There was so much alcohol in his system that when they gave him a transfusion, they had to pre-mix it with rye whisky in a special machine, or his body would have gone into shock and shut down."

The skinny handsome fellow suddenly got in my face again.

"So, you've had our cocaine, you've had our rum. Do we have to give you a fucken blowjob before you do something in return for us, eh?"

This felt like it was either a joke or serious depending on how I took it. The kid was grin-grimacing at me, pulling his lips back over his gums like some neglected horses we used to see come in to the ranch. "Cribbers," they're called. They chew on fences and suck wind to give themselves some kind of horsey thrill. They even chew on their own fucking legs, sometimes. It's awful to see. People try to cure it with round pens, electric fences, or a tight strap around the jaw, but my old man and his brothers were all of the opinion that you could never really break them of it. It's a mercy to shoot them. Maybe I could talk the others into kicking Skinny Top Hat Boy outta the band, eventually.

"Look at it this way, Tweekey — I was doing you a favour, sucking up some of that nose powder. That means there's less of it laying around to make you even more squirrel-like."

Tweekey's eyes widened in anger.

"Jacob, turn yourself down a notch for chrissakes. I just *gave* you a blowjob. Can't you *relax* a little? He's not going to get us in if we threaten him, sillypants."

Here was the Little Mother, shepherding her flock again. It worked. Jacob did a pirouette, like there was never any doubt that he was just funning.

"What would you people *do* if I got you past those gates, anyway?"

"We'd become international celebrities."

"Kidnap Jimmy Kinnock and sell him for ransom to the *Manchester Guardian*."

"There is no *Manchester Guardian* anymore."

"Then he's a dead man."

"Light off my cherry bombs in the merch tent."

"Bum smokes off [CENSORED] then fuck her in the A-hole with a dildo."

"Steal all the Inca Crafts from the craft tent and take them back to Inca-land."

"I'm 'onna get me one of those golf carts they got —"

"Me too! I'll race ya!"

"— and see how many hippies I can run over."

"Wheee! Two hundred points!"

"Hold up the guy from Junkhouse for his blow stash and do it all in the handicapped porta-potty."

"I wanna meet Rosalyn Knight."

"Yeah, because you *loooooove* her. You wanna *mar-ry* her. But you ca-an't, 'cause sheeeee's fucking straiy-yait."

"That never stopped me before!"

"Fuck you, bitch!"

"No, fuck you!"

"Wanna scrap? Let's go!"

The pretty tough girl went after the little fiddler with open handed slaps from above, but the little fiddler deftly dodged the blows, leapt surprisingly high and pulled the tall girl's leather jacket over her head like a hockey goon grabbing a jersey.

"Hey, no fair!"

The two of them went down together and started to roll around.

"Come on, fight, you fucking pussy!"

This was amusing and stimulating, but I had to get back to work.

"Thanks for the horse brutality. Here's my card. Bomb-Smuggler Entertainment. Drop me a line. We'll see what we can do about getting you in for next year."

"Thanks, Mr. Important."

"I gotta get to the After-Party."

MID-REPORT ASSESSMENT

HOLY SHIT, I JUST LOOKED UP from my scribbling for the first time in a while. There's yellow paper everywhere. It's like some giant twelve-foot canary stepped on a landmine or something. The plan was I was just going to write something clear and concise, to drive the point home about how if you really look at things from the right angle, with all the information that I was privy to, that I am not the villain of the piece. I think I said it was only going to be about twenty-five pages, and it's certainly a fair bit longer. It's gonna be a bitch to collate. Clearly gotten out of hand, like everything else in my life. For that I apologize.

I took a few minutes to look out the window just now. The sun is going down here again. Living in Vancouver these past years, I do miss these golden prairie sunsets, with their long shadows and magic light. Unless you're rich enough to live near the water in Vancouver, sunset is just like some hippie got ahold of the city's dimmer switch and the place goes from light grey to very dark grey. And nothing ever gets dry there. I have the same itching west coast fungus between my toes that I acquired when I moved out there. I know because it gets mail at my address. It sends away for homeopathic cures to try to get rid of me.

It strikes me how my life in Vancouver, with its off-kilter, sporadic rhythm of all-night deadline grant-application-writing, long jaw sessions of drinking beer out of coffee mugs at cafés on

Commercial Drive, the necessary gig attendances of various artists I have an interest in at various booze-cans, nightclubs, and theatres, the sudden naps that come on like heart attacks in the afternoon and last till the next afternoon — it's both decadent and impoverished, compared to how I grew up. When I was a kid, till my mom took us to the city, I got up at 5 a.m. to do chores: letting the chickens out, feeding and brushing the horses. I had to come home from school and do more chores. It made my body hurt. It made me very tired at the end of the day. But to and from school — and you probably won't believe this — I got to ride my own horse. That's a luxury that even a rich kid in Vancouver wouldn't be allowed. And those toffee noses are the only kids allowed to ride horses at all in that city. I've seen those private-school girls out in their English jodhpurs and hoity-toity hats on the trails near the university, the horses with their manes in cute braids, Jesus Christ. What a way to humiliate a noble, beautiful animal, making it all *nice* like that.

In Vancouver, it's true I get to do whatever, whenever, and I get to follow my muse and really make things happen. And I do relish that. I'm a scavenging urban animal now, like a raccoon. But in my first life, when I wasn't free, I was a different creature. I was fitter. I got more fresh air. Life had an even-ness about it. Even my dad's temper was tied to the seasons, the days of the week, the time of day. People who only know me the way I am now are always shocked when I reveal my rural skills. I think that's what won Colleen over to trusting me, back in the late eighties. She invited me out to her shack, an hour and a half out of town, to play me some ancient vicious Scottish postpartum depression ballads she'd just dug up from some archive and learned by heart. After I chopped about half a cord of wood for her stove, I went over and put in some braces on the corner posts of her sagging fence. Then when she was playing me the songs, right there in the middle of singing about wishing she was deep, deep under the soft, dark moss in the churchyard, sleeping close with her bonny,

bonny baby, she brought out a big red vibrator with the face of a devil and did a buzzing guitar solo with it. I guess it's overly sentimental or romantic of me to say this, but at that moment, I somehow just *knew* that sooner or later that day, that thing was going to wind up inside one, or both of us. The answer was both. And sooner. Good days.

What was my point in that? It might just be that I'm sitting here, writing all this, partly just because I'm not ready to go home. Does that make sense? Probably not. I guess I'd better get on with the damn story.

HE QUIT DRINKING

I WAS AT THE AFTER-PARTY. I was in no rush. I didn't want to look desperate. Buckwheat Zydeco wasn't even playing yet. I was just subtly, easily, socially working my way across the room towards Wren. He didn't look like he was going anywhere.

I spotted Keith Krapp. He was our go-to soundman when we first started putting on punk rock shows at the Russian Hall in Edmonton. Then when he moved to Vancouver he helped me out a lot getting the contacts I needed there. Good man. Not like other soundmen.

SOUNDMAN'S GUIDE

I ALWAYS WONDERED WHY in God's name soundmen in Canada were always the way they were. Then one time, I barged into the chickenwire booth at a place called Call the Office, in London (Ontario, emphatically *not* England), and found this strange document, in the form of tattered, faint photocopied pages bound together with masking tape. By the looks of it, it was a photocopy of a photocopy of a carbon copy, some kind of Canuck *samizdat* whose origins were lost in the mists of time. I've copied it out best I could here from memory. I tell, you it explains a lot.

"What The Fuck Do You Want?"
— A Soundman's Guide

The job of sound technician is a storied one. There are many grand traditions. Some young people — women, especially — who have recently entered the profession, fail to uphold these longstanding practices, passed down soundguy to soundguy, generation to generation. But without these traditions, we would cease to truly be soundmen, and would soon find ourselves reduced to the role of mere servants of musicians. So that this should never come to pass, the brotherhood has kept the flame of this guide alive, these many years. Keep them secret, but most of all, keep them. Live them. Be a soundguy.

1. Don't Hassle Me, I've Done This a Million Times!

Remember that you've heard everything there is to hear, and you are too cool to care. Your lack of interest in music and the world around you should confound even the most jaded hipster musician. For instance, in cases when the period that you feel is appropriate for soundcheck has elapsed, and you want to go have dinner, but you find that the band is still not happy with the sound, the following phrase should always be employed: "Don't worry, the room'll sound totally different when there's people here." Always speak the phrase with the proper, provoking, sense of nonchalance. If delivered properly, it should demoralize musicians by implying that a) the whole forty-five-minute process of soundcheck was a meaningless charade, and b) that your lassitude is just a preview of things to come!

2. Set It, Then Forget It!

There's only one acceptable, professional way to deal with situations where you're asked to do sound for something weird that you don't like: Put the levels at a certain arbitrary setting, and then, you know, go for a smoke in the alley, or to do some blow backstage, or call a friend on the payphone at the back of the bar. Whatever. When you hear the faint echoes of screaming feedback emanating from the stage, don't *rush* back — finish your smoke, visit the men's room for a dump, and then maybe — maybe — have a poke round the board to see what you can see. Or not!

3. Fake Adjustment

This is a neat trick that provides endless amusement, which you can brag about later to your buddies behind the bar after closing time: Let's say that the singer, or mandolin player, or whoever, asks you to turn him up in the monitor, or lower the reverb effect, or something. Instead of actually changing the setting, *you pretend* to adjust the knob, but actually *do nothing* to the sound. If the musician gives up in despair and thanks you for making the adjustment, laugh to yourself about how stupid they are for not noticing that it's *exactly the same!*

4. Road Stories

Remember that time you went on the road as a roadie or monitor guy for a semi-famous professional band, for about two weeks, fifteen years ago? Make sure that you drop that band's name within the first seven minutes of meeting anyone at all, ever. Tell that funny story about the time you did the Fake Adjustment (*see above*) to the asshole lead singer.

5. Apparel

You got into this business to distinguish yourself from the "suits" and working stiffs who have to get up early in the morning and put on suits, and other work uniforms. So don't let the Man tell you what to wear. Always, always, always wear faded jeans, preferably acid-washed, and a ratty old rock T-shirt, preferably from that tour fifteen years ago that you did with that semi-famous band. If it gets extremely hot on stage, you may strip down to a stained wife-beater undershirt. Remember that these are your work clothes, so there is no need to wash them more than once a month at the very most. Top it all off with a baseball cap. This baseball cap should be a promotional item from a huge international beverage company that makes beer that tastes like piss. You may be tempted to imitate the bravado of those youngsters who are wearing the ballcap backwards these days, but if you have a ratty pony tail, don't waste it — make sure that it pops saucily out the back, between the strap and the netting. In this manner you achieve the welcome eye-shading of the hat brim, but also demonstrate to the world that you are wild and cannot be tamed.

6. Fanny Packs

Fanny packs are those little nylon bags that wrap around your waist, and hang on your bum. You can use them to hold useless cables that you tell yourself you'll one day repair, or weed, or gum. Women find them overpoweringly attractive. Be sure that when you wear the fanny pack hanging over your bum, it doesn't obscure your ass crack, which should always be evident for all to see whenever you bend over or crouch in the course of your duties. This may seem like a burden, but never forget: you have a responsibility to be a credibility-defying, breathing, walking cliché.

7. Musicians

The biggest drawback to doing sound for bands is of course that bands have musicians in them. Try to remember that musicians are mostly just a bunch of whiny little punks who aren't even old enough to remember *real* music, especially the band you toured with fifteen years ago, and they should be treated with as much condescension as possible. If a musician makes a request for help or information, try to feign deafness and walk away. Another good tactic is to look them dead in the eye and say something like "Well, where do you *think* it would be?" If you must directly answer a question from a musician, always remember that answers should in every instance be preceded by the Long, Exasperated Sigh *and then* the Incredulous Eye-Roll (*see diagrams*).

8. Women

Women. Where do they come from? What do they want? This is a difficult subject, which has puzzled some of our greatest philosophers. But like it or not, there will be times when you will have to deal with non-waitress women in your workplace. Always remember that female musicians, in particular, don't know Nothing about Nothing. And because women don't even know what they're talking about, make it a point of principle to ignore any request they make, especially if these requests involve technical elements of sound. If a woman surprises you by playing her instrument well, don't be caught off guard without the important and time-honoured phrase, "Not bad — for a girl. Haw, haw." (*Try rehearsing that phrase now.*) Wives, spouses, partners, and girlfriends should exclusively be referred to as "Old Ladies," as in, "One way or another, this soundcheck's gonna be over in fifteen minutes, 'cause I told the Old Lady I'd be home in time fer supper, and I wanna have time to give 'er one. Heh heh."

HE QUIT DRINKING, CONTINUED (SORRY FOR INTERRUPTION)

SORRY, I JUST HAD TO throw that in there, to let you know how special Keith Krapp is. He's like the opposite of the above. I have a deep affection for the guy. So there he was at the After-Party, and he had something dark red in a glass, and he was halfway between me and Richard Wren. It's one of my idiosyncrasies that I try to police people who've officially quit alcohol forever, to keep them on the straight and narrow. It's to counteract my unearned, unfair reputation for corrupting people.

I ambled up and put my large arm around him.

"Keith! What's that you got there? I thought I heard you quit drinkin'."

"Campbell Ouiniette. My favourite Big Hairy Monster. How you keeping?"

"I'm on a roll. You're not back on the sauce, are you?"

"On a roll. So I hear. Your new, ah, 'finds' are the talk of the festival. Still stirring up the shit, eh? I think I've got one of them, the big-boned kid, at my stage tomorrow."

"Don't try to change the subject. So you fallen off the wagon or what?"

"It's a virgin Caesar, Cam. Taste it."

"Yech. No, I'll take your word for it. So you're a born-again virgin. Good for you."

We clinked glasses and looked each other directly in the eyes as we drank, in the eastern European manner.

"Yeah. You know, a man has a drink limit of drinks in his life. I drank my limit."

"I remember I used to be able to pretty much set my watch by you, 'cause you always fell down and passed out, wherever you were, at exactly 4:30 in the a.m. In your trademark green trenchcoat."

"Loved that trenchcoat. Loved it. That was my protection. It always felt so nice and temperate in the evening in Vancouver."

"It *felt* that way 'cause you were drunk."

"'Cause I was drunk. Right — but then when I woke up in the morning …"

"And you were freezing and wet."

"Even on a warm night, even in summer — the damn dew would get me. In the morning, I'd wake up all wet and shivering, covered in condensation, on somebody's lawn."

"So that was what the trenchcoat was for."

"That was what the trenchcoat was for. But one morning, I actually woke up *in the gutter*, still wet and shivering, even in my trusty trenchcoat. So I was like, this is too much. I have got to do *something* about this."

"So that's when you quit drinking, eh?"

"Naw, I started wearing *two* trenchcoats, so I wouldn't get so cold. I quit eight years after that, when I lost my left eye to diabetes. Cheers."

He looked me hard in the eye, and I could see the glass, now I was looking for it, as we clinked glasses again.

"Well, that reminds me, my beer's just about empty. I'll catch you at the Ironwood stage tomorrow?"

"Sure. Your boy need anything special for his balalaika?"

"Kobza, it's called. Balalaika's Russian. He hates it when you get those mixed up. No. He just uses a regular 57 instrument mic, I believe. Make sure you have the popsock on the vocal mic washed after he performs. He's an emotional guy, so he tends to spray bits of his latest meal all over it when he sings."

"Right. Take care of yourself there, Cam."

"Yeah. See you tomorrow."

I headed for the bar.

THE UPSHOT

AFTER A QUICK FORTIFYING tequila shot, I was ready to move in on Wren.

There he was, holding up the wall with some kind of clear drink in his hand. Couldn't tell if it was booze. *I'll make sure that's taken care of, my friend*, I thought to myself. He was chatting enthusiastically with Mykola, gesticulating with the drink. The boy was clearly terrified, staring at his boots, wishing he was back in his room scarfing perogies, no doubt. This was the moment. Time to go in for the kill.

"Hey, Campbell! Campbell!"

Shit.

Leslie Stark ploughed like a little tank through the crowd, totally heedless of the many people whose drinks she was spilling as she jostled towards me. Why should she care anyway — it was her festival, and it was a success, the numbers were good, so no one was complaining. Except me, on the inside. Outwardly, I was friendly.

"Leslie! Fuck! The numbers looked good today, eh?"

"Yeah. Listen, I need to talk with you up in the office suite."

"Sure, I'll be right up there, gotta go check something with Mykola here." I had been continuing to drift in that direction as we spoke.

"Great to meet you. Good job in the workshop this afternoon. You've really got something that's a bit different. Can I borrow Campbell for a few minutes? He'll catch up with you later."

Mykola raised his eyebrows, breathed slowly through his nose and irritated us all as we waited for him to say what of course we all knew he had to say anyway to the A.D. of the festival.

"Ummmm, sure, yeah. Thank you."

I slipped a quick, firm, friendly handshake in on Wren, "Good to meet you, I'm Campbell Ouiniette. We met earlier. Got some stuff I'd like to discuss with you."

"Hi! Yeah, great. Nice to see you." Agh. The non-committal "Yeah, great." Like getting punched in the lower intestines with a pitchfork. God, if only she would just have left me alone with him and the tequila. I *knew* I would have him. But there she was, steering me by the elbow toward the door, and then the elevator. What could I do? Fuck all, that's what. I'd have some work to do when I got back down to the party.

SHE CLOSED THE DOOR OF the hotel suite she was using as an onsite office, and went to sit behind the desk, motioning to the chair in front of it.

"Have a seat."

She linked her fingers and laid them on the desk in front of me like a closed castle drawbridge.

"So."

I figured the whiskey could still be good for something. I yanked it out of the robe and plonked it on the desk.

She laughed, "What is this? A kick-back?"

"You got any glasses?"

"In the bathroom."

I filled up an obscene tumbler-full for each of us, and offered my usual toast.

"Nice driveway."

"Cheers."

She put away half of it. The woman can drink, I'll give her that. Her eyes rolled up a bit in her head for a sec, but then they were back to fixing me with that crocodile stare.

"So where's my Sunday headliner?"

Time to do my schtick.

"Fuck!" I screamed, waving my robe-clad arms wildly. I always start with that when I'm caught out. It unsettles people. They think they've got me in a position where I should be kind of squirming and politely hemming and hawing, and instead I counter with a flaming burst of negative emotion and noise. It puts them off balance, especially Canadians.

"Fuck! Fuck! FUCK! The woman won't return my calls or emails, I've tried her fucking relatives up in the goddamn Arctic Circle, and she's nowhere to be found. I am really getting fed up with this bullshit."

Leslie said nothing. Took another drink of Scotch.

I blathered on. "I'm telling you, I'm just about ready to drop this artist. Reliability is a real issue here. Fuck, you know, like they say, 90 percent of success is just showing up."

"Mmm."

"I guess the question is, what are we gonna do?" Always make it a "we" problem, is my strategy.

"Right."

"Look, here's how I see it. Athena's never totally fucked off on a show before. It's true, she smokes a little weed sometimes, and recently, maybe the sudden success has gone to her head, so she's been going a little prima donna on me lately. But she's never actually skipped out on the main show before."

"She's caused quite a sensation. Lot of people are asking me about her."

"So my thinking is, she'll probably come *waltzing* in here tomorrow, be like, 'Oh, I didn't know I had to do *workshops* at this festival. Anyway, I've got this great new costume, my cousin made it for me,' and be all set to go. Or maybe not. Maybe she's sick. Who knows. She's had some health problems. She can't eat wheat. Adjusting to the southern diet."

Leslie drank again, but was silent, staring at me. It occurred to me that she looked uncannily like a little kid watching the elephants at the circus.

"Anyway, but what if she doesn't show? We still have the main stage 9 p.m. slot to fill on Sunday. That is a major thing. So obviously, that's my responsibility."

"Uh-unh."

"So if Athena's not there, my thinking is, we've got two killer singer-songwriters and a DJ, superior artists in their own right. We need to fill that time, Mykola and Jenny have been total sensations this weekend already; everybody's talking about them."

"Yeah, I got several audience complaints about both of them."

"Gezacktly!" I shouted. There was nothing more that needed to be said — between us two fans of challenging music — about how great that was.

"No, yeah, they are quite good. Original stuff. Really charismatic, both of them. She's got a great voice, and Mykola's got at least two good songs there."

That's Leslie when she *likes* somebody.

"So it's agreed, then. I'll head down and tell 'em they better hit the old fart sack sooner than later so they can really nail it tomorrow on the main stage."

"Yeah, no, that's not gonna happen, Campbell. That's silly."

No time to waste. Tried to get my wisdom out there. "Leslie —"

She was laughing now as she cut me off. "Campbell, you think I don't *know* that Athena's off with Pixie-fuck-face, the fucking Iceland world popstar on some fucking giant tour? It was in the *New York Times* music section, you asshole. It don't take a brick wall."

"What the *fuck? That bitch! She fucked me over!*" Important to feign surprise here, just for propriety's sake.

Leslie laughed harder.

"Campbell, I fucking love you, man. You're awesome."

"Leslie! We're both awesome. So what about having the band guys do the set? It'll be a sensation, it'll be the talk of the circuit. You'll get the credit for being the most adventurous A.D. in the country."

"I'll be the most *fired* A.D. in the fucking country. No, what's gonna happen is Don McLean will play an extra twenty minutes, so he can do a third song before 'Starry, Starry Night' and 'American Pie' and the Australians will do an encore."

"*What?* That's bullshit! A fucking has-been playing a song that never made any sense in the first place, and some fucking *Australians*, singing about the joy of sunshine and ripping off the Aborigines? *That's* what you're going to replace *Athena Amarok* with? You've got a challenging artist in that slot. People are expecting to be challenged. There's going to be total outrage out there. It's nuts!"

"Outrage would be if I put a couple of unknown freaks singing about tit-licking and genocide on the main stage Sunday night. Those pretty Australians pull up to every folk festival with a fucking Hertz Truck full of CDs. You have no notion of what the audience is really looking for, Campbell, and I love you for that. Don't push your luck. I'm kinda pissed at you for this whole Athena thing, but I'm going to be incredibly generous and let you hold on to the advance I sent you in March, and I'm not gonna sue you or have you charged with fraud, although I should. You're lucky that I'm an incredibly nice person. I'll even let you take the Scotch with you, although after what you've done to me here, it's rightfully mine."

There was nothing to say. I was silently dignified. I stood up. I drained my glass in a gulp.

I looked her square in the eye, and raised my right hand.

"I swear to you, on my daughter's life, I did not know that Athena had gone off with some Icelandic disco yodeller."

"Right on, whatever. I'll see you down at the party, you big lying cocksucker."

THE HAIL MARY PASS

I LEFT LESLIE'S ROOM, STUNNED, with one thing on my mind: the Hail Mary pass. I had to find Richard Wren, get him drunk, and solidify some kind of deal. Then I'd still have my prize for the weekend to bring home. As I calculated it, he was totally primed by the workshop — he was ripe for the picking. I know how to handle the English. Especially the classy ones. You kind of go cowboy on them, talk about horses and guns and shit (all of which I know a great deal about, having grown up on a horse ranch). It wakes up the kid in them, gets them ready to say "yes" to anything you have in mind.

In the elevator I was rehearsing my best lines, getting ready to handle him. Unfortunately I was feeling a little dark after the conversation with Leslie and every time I tried to think of horses, I had this little problem where I couldn't stop thinking about the time when I was ten and I pulled a shotgun on my pap in the kitchen to stop him from hitting my mom and he disarmed me and threw me to the floor, and those thoughts were just leading me to thinking about the way the house and the chicken yard and my saddle horse looked as my mom drove us away in her old Volkswagen Beetle with the hole in the floor a couple days later when my dad was safely passed out. I'd had to look away from everything I was leaving and concentrate on watching the muddy slushy mush of the dirt road passing by through the floor-hole.

BUT I KNEW THIS WAS THE TIME of destiny, and I had one shot and I had to make it count. So I gave my head about ten shakes, and by the time the elevator got me down to the party-room floor, I was back where I needed to be and ready to dance. I have that ability, the power to turn my feelings around and point them in the other direction. My Herculean emotional strength had me in a space where I was actually now absolutely set and looking forward to my seduction battle with Wren. I felt that as colleagues in the same crazy, up-and-down business, he and I could commiserate together, and I could commune with the old pro about the nature of being a Manager, of singing your life through other people. In my bag, I fingered the "Co-Management Agreement Contract" papers I'd made up back in Vancouver.

Out the elevator, through the lobby. The Supersonic Grifters had insinuated themselves onto a couch there, before the "passes only" area started, and they were playing some folk song about smashing machinery, at quadruple the speed it was normally played. Old Utah Phillips was sitting by on the arm of the couch, smiling upon them like an anarchist Santa Claus. I could see a couple hotel security dicks moving in their direction. Over to the left, some paramedics were loading a girl with heatstroke or alcohol poisoning or an overdose or something onto a gurney.

Up the steps, flashing my pass. Into the ballroom, past the lineup for chili.

I scanned the room, looking for a white-haired Englishman.

Mexican cowboy band on stage. The party heating up. Volunteer security personnel doing silly-named shooters at the bar.

There he was. Literally holding court at a corner table. Various hangers-on, hopefuls, and fans trolling for inside gossip surrounded him. A carafe of red wine before him. Good. How could you tell he was powerful? He was *smoking* with impunity, indoors, in Canada. And no one saying a thing.

I strode toward the cocktail bar to get my soon-to-be new friend a special cocktail.

There was a growling sound from behind me. I turned and a chubby little blond hippie girl danced past me, giggling in her Thai wrap skirt. Mykola was on his hands and knees, chasing her, snapping his teeth.

"*Stop* biting my ankles!" she laughed, not particularly running away.

"*Rrrrr*. Oh hi, Cam!"

"Looks like you're feeling a bit less nervous, Mykola. Having a good festival?"

"Oh, yeah, thank you."

He climbed up a chair to his feet, and offered a paw to shake.

"Everything went just like you said! You were right! Did you hear? Richard Wren has invited Jenny and me to London. England!"

"Oh, really?"

"This could be our big break! Thanks, Cam. Thanks so much for this. I really owe you. Hey, did you hear the little fiddle-playing dyke girl in the busking band outside the gates?"

"I don't suppose he said anything about talking to me about London, first, did he?"

He looked surprised. It hadn't even crossed his mind.

"Well, um, he's right over there if you wanna talk to him."

"That's what I'll do."

"Okay, great. See you later, man." He dropped down on all fours and crawled off to the beat of the Mexican cowboy music.

"... BUT THE THING WAS, and I told them to their faces, 'Listen mate, the best part of your band just lost his mind to LSD. I don't care how much money's involved, I just don't find it creatively interesting, you know?"

"Hello, there, Mister Wren. Thought I'd bring you over something special. Mind if I sit down?"

"Please do — oh you're the fellow who's with Mykola and Jenny. Bloody brilliant. Brilliant stuff."

"This here is a Caesar. It was actually invented right here at the Westin Hotel in Calgary. When I tell people in Europe what it's made of, they usually don't believe me."

"Oh God, it's not that awful drink made of clam juice or summat?"

"I guess you've been to Canada before."

"Since before you were born, my son. Don't really have to go at this point, of course. Just love the scenery here, though. The big skies, wide open spaces where you can breathe." Big intake of breath. "Bit of a busman's holiday, really."

"Where's the Brave Hero of the British Left?"

"Hmm?"

"Jimmy. Your actual client."

"Oh, yeah, Jimmy's gone to bed."

"Jimmy doesn't stay up and party?"

"Not for ages. Wants his voice to be in good shape. Feels he owes it to the people who pay their hard-earned wages to see him."

"Not very rock 'n' roll."

"No, I suppose I'm probably a bit more flamboyant than him these days. That's a bit pathetic, really. Hah."

"I hear he lives on a sheep farm now."

"Yeah, it's not a sheep farm anymore, though. Just a big piece of land. Big in terms of England."

"Not very socialistic, being a big landowner."

"Yeah, he has trouble with that. The rabble-rouser in him feels it's a bit wrong, really. He's afraid his daughter's growing up talking posh. What can he do? The poor bastard's rich as Croesus. All my fault, I s'pose."

"You sound amused. You don't have any qualms like that?"

"Qualms? Qualms? No qualms on me. I grew up posh, as a matter of fact. Went to Rugby as a day boy, didn't I? *Orando Laborando.*"*

---

* I looked that up. It means, "By praying, by working." It's the Motto of Rugby School, *alma mater* of many British luminaries, including the great Victorian hero, Brigadier-General Harry Paget Flashman, VC, KCB, KCIE. He's an ancestor of mine, on my father's side, funnily enough.

"You're a champagne socialist?"

"It's my considered political position that I should have a right to drink champagne now and then. As a socialist, I just advocate champagne for everybody else, as well."

"Well, that sounds perfectly consistent. Let me buy us a bottle of champagne."

There was still *just* enough room on the third credit card for that.

WE CHATTED ON: MUSIC, politics, travel, the idiosyncrasies of musicians. He told me about the time he had to bribe a jetlagged Chuck Berry out of his sudden refusal to play a British rock festival by gifting him with the ownership papers of the Rolls that had brought him from Heathrow. I told him about the time I got fired from emceeing South Country Fair when I announced from the stage, during a summer prairie lightning outbreak, "Ladies and gentlemen, we're experiencing an electrical storm. Would all the hippies and Australians please place their hands on the tall metal swing set in the centre of the field." He laughed. He was laughing at my jokes.

All the hangers-on had dropped away. They could see this was a meeting of minds that should not be fucked with. So after the champagne, in the spirit of thrift, we sucked up all the booze that had been left lying unattended on the table. Then Wren had a thought: "Hang on a minute. Forgot I had this!" He reached into his satchel and brought out a bottle of eighteen-year-old Scotch whose name neither of us could pronounce by that point in the evening.

I could feel it. This was the unmistakable sign of comraderie and bonhomie and good feeling. I could feel the co-management papers pressing against my chest. I had charmed the snake, and now it was time to climb it into the clouds, like a Swami in a Bob Hope movie.

"I wanted to talk to you about Mykola and Jenny. I understand that you've invited them to London."

"I told them, they've absolutely *got* to get out of Can-a-der if they ever want to get anywhere. Told them to stop by, we'll put them up in the spare room. They're absolutely wonderful. Can't promise anything, but there's a real possibility we may want to work with them."

Yes, yes, yes. Strike at once!

"Well, you know, I'm their manager. I thought maybe we could discuss that a bit more. I have some ideas about how we might co-operate."

Wren blinked, then trained a very direct, very unclouded gaze at me. It held my eyes effortlessly. He took hold of the bottle and poured himself a couple of fingers. His motion was smooth.

"Sorry, I don't follow."

"I'm saying we could work together pretty well here. I'd be the one who — "

"— Oh, no, sorry, that's what's called a 'co-management' deal."

Geez, thanks for the remedial music-biz lesson.

"We don't do co-management deals. Our artists are like family to us. We do everything for them. Taxes, insurance, we even pay their telly license for them. We used to practically change Jimmy's nappies for 'im. Still do, some days."

He was so so so *nonchalant* about it.

"No, if we did decide to take them on, of course we'd buy you out. Small cash settlement."

"Small cash settlement?"

"Can't keep what doesn't want to stay, after all, mate. If you love something, set it free, et cetera. But obviously it's much too early to say." He sipped his whiskey and turned slightly to watch the dance floor behind my shoulder. Change of scenery.

My first instinct was of course, violence. But then I thought, *No, you're better than that, Cam. You can't sink to the level of this arrogant, calculating bastard.*

But then I just decided to go with my first instinct. I'm a big believer in that.

Here's some advice: It's much better, when you want to break a glass or bottle for the purpose of attacking someone, to grab an empty receptacle, rather than one that's still got liquid in it. Because the spraying of the liquid, especially if the liquid is red, can be both distracting and needlessly lubricating. The last thing you want is a slippery weapon.

And if you're going to attack someone with, say, a broken cocktail glass, you should make sure that you break it right on the first try, because if you take three tries to do it and fail, that allows enough time for Big Dave MacLean the Winnipeg bluesman and his big beefy bass player to notice what you're up to, put their hands on your shoulders and say "Why don't you come out with us for a smoke, Cam?" in a way that suggests that you don't really have any choice.

In my defence, I wasn't really going to cut him. I was just going to hold the broken glass to his throat, and tell him to leave my people the fuck alone.

My thinking is, I normally would have easily been able to break the glass, so I must have subconsciously been holding myself back from doing something that might have hurt Mykola and Jenny's chances for their big break. That's what I think I was doing, really.

EJECTED

BIG DAVE AND HIS BASSIST sat me down fairly insistently on the curb of the parking lot. He shoved a cancer stick in my mouth, unlit, at a crazy oblique angle, and shoved his face in mine.

"I don't want to see you back in there till you've cooled off, Cam. Is that understood? If you run back in there looking for trouble, you know what we'll have to do, don't you?"

"*Rngh.*"

"Okay then," said Big Dave.

Rosalyn Knight was in mid-anecdote, smoking nearby with a coven of cackling, similarly louche ladies in pretty thrift-store dresses with various stains and artfully mussed hair.

"Oh, Christ, and sure enough, they come right up to the stage, and they're, 'Like, you mind if we jam along with your set, man?' It's unbelievable."

"What did you do?"

"Oh well, I just said, 'Oh I would love to *jam*, but unfortunately, both of my parents were killed by bongos, so they're very traumatic for me.'"

Big Dave turned to her and motioned toward me.

"You ladies, keep an eye on him?"

"Uh, yeah, of course. He tries to go back in, I'll do my Tae Kwon Do on him." Rosalyn made a few perfunctory martial-art moves in my direction, cigarette in one hand, wineglass in the other. The ladies cackled some more as Big Dave and his buddy went in.

I slumped down, putting my face in my hands, inadvertently crushing my smoke.

"Uh-oh. Somebody's having a shitty night."

"I'm an idiot."

"Oh, don't say that. It takes all the fun out of pointing it out to you. You don't look so good, Scampbell. If you hadn't ripped off so many of my friends, I'd be feeling really sorry for you right now. Maybe you should call it a morning."

"Fuck. Why is the music bizness so fucking fucked up?"

"Well, my theory is, there's smoke and mirrors in every business. But when the actual *product* is smoke and mirrors, it makes it that much trickier to know what the fuck's going on. Of course you wouldn't know anything about that. Because you're just a simple fucking smoke machine."

"How do you deal with it?"

"My needs are simple. I like to make up songs. I like to put on a show. I like travelling, hanging around with my dysfunctional friends."

"Don't you care about Making It? Being a Star?"

"Nooo, I'm totally above that. I'm completely zen with the universe, man."

"Ok, but what if you never get there, never get where you're trying to go?"

She took a long, dramatic drag, and said, on the exhale, "Fuck it."

I sat and thought.

DRUNKEN SELF-SABOTAGE

IT'S TRUE, I DRINK A LOT. Perhaps some people might call me an Alcoholic, but in the regions of eastern Europe where I've been touring since the early nineties, where we get plied with *palinka* at the end of *breakfast*, just as a matter of *common courtesy*, to "wake us up" before we hit the road, I am merely a human being, a pedestrian. The world is a fucked-up place. As far as I'm concerned, if you can go through life and you're actually paying attention to what's going on, and the stuff you see *doesn't* make you feel like you need a drink — well, as far as I'm concerned, that would make you a psychopathically callous individual.

I used to drink with a doctor of psychology in the basement bar of a university student union building. He told me — while ogling the undergraduates of both genders without a hint of discretion — that his clinical definition for addiction was as follows: a situation where something you do on a regular basis is actually making your life worse, not better. He further said that, in the end, everybody's got to make that calculation for themselves. Sounds about right to me.

Obviously, a lesion-covered heroin addict in downtown Regina is not doing *better* for being a heroin addict. Unless the heroin makes that heroin addict forget for seven blessed minutes that when he was nine years old he watched his stepfather rape his sister. If that heroin addict calculates that the seven minutes of forgetting is worth the lesions and all the other stuff, who the fuck am I to say?

But yes, it's true, there have been instances where I have probably harmed myself, or my "career." I don't normally talk about these
instances, simply because it's bad for business, and not because I
can't admit when I'm wrong, which is a complete falsehood.

There was that time that I had the charge of some young
quirky punky kids from the bourgeois West Side of Vancouver,
taking them on a tour around Czech Republic, when I wound up
puking up a big goulash meal with some mulled wine, beer, and
vodka in Wenceslas Square at four in the morning. People talk as
if everything was fixed after the Velvet Revolution, but the police
were still as corrupt and nasty as ever. When I couldn't pay the
beat cops their bribe, they handed me a mop and bucket and made
me clean up my own mess. That was an operation with several
false starts, if you know what I mean, and each time my stomach
revolted at the smell of its own contents, the boys in black would
give me a couple of solid shots with their nightsticks. A few of
their civilian countrymen stood around to jeer them on. It was the
late nineties by then, and after several years of openness, I guess
the charm of playing host to Westerners' pig-wild cheap Easyjet
alcoholidays had worn off a bit.

Unfortunately I lost sight of the kids I was supposed to be shepherding around, and they missed several shows after being taken
under the wing of a unibrowed Canadian bar impresario named
Glen, from Burnaby. I did finally find them in a brothel in Brno, a
recently-converted Communist Pioneer Youth for Healthy Living
Centre. They were rather grey from lack of sleep but otherwise
mostly unharmed. I never did find out which side of the brothel
transactions they'd been enlisted in, and I thought it insensitive to
pry too much. I managed to talk the big moustachioed men wearing Confederate flag T-shirts who were cleaning old-fashioned Colt
pistols in the front room into letting the boys go, and we even got
to the gig on time that night, but they never really wanted to work
with me again. I will say in my defence, though, that the album they
wrote and recorded after they got home was much darker, harsher,

more infused with the real pain of experience than their previous work. They'd had some of the Kerrisdale taken out of them.

There was also that Norwegian band that I brought out to Canada to open on tour for Cole Dixon's old hard rock outfit. They were big in their home country, and I was going to get them rolling in North America. That turned out to be a pipe dream because of Cole's abilities as a poker player. He's a strange man. I've seen him finish a gig at 2 a.m., get back to the hotel room at three, and be on the phone seeing if there's any casinos open in town. Then he'll head out and play Texas Hold 'Em till ten in the morning, get picked up and sleep as the bus rolls, all the way to soundcheck, like a fuckin' vampire in a cowboy hat. I guess somebody told him he needed to have a career to fall back on in case music didn't work out, and he picked card shark.

Cole was stringing those Norwegians along the whole tour, "teaching" them how to play poker each night after the shows, with toothpicks as chits. I knew what he was doing. I should have known on the second-to-last night of the tour when Cole bought me a "present" of two great big bottles of Maker's Mark, that was the night he was gonna make his move. It was so easy. They'd been "winning" all these toothpicks off him for the last week, and several times they'd suggested they all play for real money to "make it interesting." Cole, being a gentleman, had of course always politely declined. 'Cause he knew I was watching him, and I would have stepped in.

But then that evening, because of Cole's gift, I was the worse for wear, some fat chick from Brooks, Alberta, was trying in vain to fuck my insensate form in the back of the tour bus while he lined the squareheads* up for slaughter. When one of them brought up

---

* "Squarehead" is a little-known racial slur on Norwegians. I try to make a point of learning the slanderous terms for every national group I encounter. I've never found a satisfyingly nasty one for Australians, though. "Nation of convicts" just doesn't hold any sting in my book. They're more like a nation of unquestioning, incurious prison guards, really.

the idea of playing for dough again, I bet he hemmed and hawed a couple of times before "reluctantly" agreeing to humour them.

The next morning, I made him give them back their instruments, but he held on to most of their *kroners*. I think they always suspected me of setting them up, but I honestly just failed to be there when they needed to be protected.

Not all my alcohol-related failures were sins of omission, of course. There was the time at the festival in northern Saskatchewan where, suspecting that the emcee had stolen my tequila, I strode onstage as he was doing a "lost child" announcement and demanded it back (the tequila, not the child), shoving him, knocking him into a speaker column that was not sufficiently fastened, which thus toppled over onto some overeager Wailin' Jenny fans, who I imagine repented somewhat that they had fought their neighbours so jealously to be right up at the front. That's one of the fests where I now have to use a false name when sending artist packages.

And if I hadn't been pretty ginned up, I probably wouldn't have thought it was a good idea to drop a dime with Canada Immigration at Vancouver International Airport on that English political folk band that tried to skip out on paying me my commission. But they did get home, eventually, after the investigation exonerated them of the charges. Wasn't too good for my rep with the limeys, though.

And I have in truth had to change cities from time to time, in order to evade bar tabs that had metastasized into figures so large that they could simply no longer be contemplated. Several pretty decent establishments may have even had to close under the weight of them. I admit that. And of course there's been the odd house fire that may or may not have been caused by drunkenly knocked-over late-night candles, and the times when slurred speech led to horrific misunderstandings involving the similarities between words, like "druid" and "jewed"; and "jugular" and "drug dealer," and a few stepped-on and stepped-through musical instruments, and of course, the incidents with the vehicles, including my somewhat ill-advised attempt to found a rental van company ...

Okay, so surveying it all now, in some ways I understand how people accuse me of being a useless, drunken bum. I understand if you feel that way, Love.

Still, when a man is tested, he has two choices: He can give up, or he can stand up. So after a decent interval, I stood up, ready to sneak past Big Dave and go and try a new approach to Wren. Yes, I'd been defeated. Yes, I'd been outmanoeuvred before I'd even really begun the journey to Calgary. Yes, I had no idea what to do to fix the situation and ingratiate myself into a negotiation, given the fact that it was certainly arguable that just twenty minutes previously I'd tried to cut the man's throat, but I felt confident that once I got in there and got close to Wren, my Manager Brain would kick in. After all, I'd figured out ways around tougher problems than this.

CRUCIAL MOMENT

I CRUISED PAST THE SECURITY volunteers, calling to an imaginary person beyond the rope, waving my pass. By this point in the evening, the security guys were close to as far gone as I was. Maybe more, since my tolerance is pretty heroic. I was determined to take that one last shot at making something work with Wren. I knew that everything came down to this moment, when I was called upon to do the Truly Impossible. It was the Ultimate Test.

RESULT

BUT OF COURSE WHEN I GOT IN, he'd already left. So there was
nothing to do but drink.

INTERMITTENT NIGHT

As I SAID, I'M NOT SOMEONE who claims to be perfect. I do admit my flaws, my mistakes. So I'm willing to concede that after that, I probably did hit the sauce a little too hard. I don't have a full accounting of every minute of every hour I spent after the crushing realization that there would be no second chance with Wren. I think of myself as a positive person, so I really tried not to let the facts of the situation depress me. I know that it was only a few minutes after I came back into the ballroom and saw that Wren was gone that I did jump up on stage with Buckwheat Zydeco and insist that we sing "Beast of Burden" together. He really does a stunning version of that song, and I know all the words.

I know that there were words between me and Jenny Reid at one point, because I remember her hitting me in the face pretty hard. I think I asked her why lesbians were so angry all the time. Jenny brought up the salient possibility that "Maybe lesbians are only angry all the time around *you.*" and, with her impeccable rhythm, timed the "you" to coincide with the impact of her right-hand haymaker. Even while I was reeling backwards from the punch, I was congratulating myself on having chosen such a talented person for the band. I really do know how to pick musicians.

Also, it may have seemed that I was making a pass at the jolly buxom blonde who was hanging out with Mykola for the night, but I swear that was just in jest. I was *satirizing* drunken, lecherous, grabby behaviour, rather than earnestly engaging in it.

And I believe that it was after *that* when I made the collect call to Athena's cellphone in London, and demanded that she fly standby to Calgary to resurrect my reputation. I know I tried various strains of persuasive rhetoric, but to no avail. I do clearly remember the last part of that conversation, because it involved Athena promising that the next time she saw me, she was going to vise my jaws open and shit down my throat. Yes, I'm pretty sure I recall that correctly.

Then there's a dark period, and I remember leaning on the wall of the lobby, and suddenly feeling very hungry, and seeing the sign for the coffee shop.

The Early Risers were having breakfast. When you're a Late Nighter, and you go all the way round to the point where you start seeing Early Risers, you should probably just avoid those cold, bright-eyed strange people like the plague, but somehow as I made my way into the coffee shop, my better instincts had deserted me. I spotted Stan Rogers' Widow sitting with some young volunteer girl, or maybe it was her daughter from a later marriage or something.

Stan Rogers' Widow is kind of the figurehead of the Stan Rogers Festival, a folkie gathering that happens every July in Canso, Nova Scotia. They always have a heavier-than-usual help-ing of diddlee-dee-ers and earnest, clichéd white folksingers, et cet-era. That's why one year, when they were in danger of losing some of their government grants on account of the lack of Canadian Cultural Mosaic Variety in their lineup, I had been brought in as a pinch-hitting programmer, to helpfully supply a few exotic ele-ments, like a Gamelon orchestra, a Japanese Kodo lady who used giant cockroaches as improvisational percussion, and a ninety-four-year-old yodelling cowboy, for good measure.

Which is to say that I wasn't a stranger to Stan Rogers' Widow when I sat myself down and proceeded to discuss with her the merits of her choice of "Amazing Grace" as the Grand Finale song for her festival. The Grand Finale is when all the artists gather in a crowd on the main stage, late Sunday night. They link arms, sway and sing, Kumbaya-style. Look, my point still remains — "Amazing Grace" is a Christian hymn, which alienates a lot of people who don't subscribe to that set of beliefs. Not just lapsed Satanists such as myself, but Atheists, people of the Hebrew persuasion, et cetera. The Ghanaian band I helped book in were fucking Animists, for God's sake — what the fuck do they care about some benighted pissant jumped-up sea shanty by some syphilitic slave-ship captain, anyway?

I mean, even Rogers himself, that bald Fake Newfie from Taranna Onterrible, didn't have much use for the Church, as far as I could see. Why not use one of his own fucking ditties? Have the whole fucking stage of World Beat-ers, third-rate Canadian electric blues-guitar wheedlee-wheedlers, irritating potato-munching racist psychotic pee-obsessed fiddlers and lesbian-separatist strummers, all join hands and sing "I'm a broken man on the Halifax Pier"? Wouldn't that at least fit the occasion? So you can see why I got a little passionate about it, obviously. It matters what song you sing. It matters. I'm sure that the Good Widow understood. I mean, she kept nodding at me. But it's true that when I get excited, after imbibing, I tend to kind of emphasize the sibilant consonants, and that can result in a certain amount of precipitation, I admit that, but I still hold it to be inaccurate and unfair for people to start instantly spreading the word from table to table about how somehow "Campbell Ouiniette just spat on Stan Rogers's widow!" I took great exception to that. And I still do.

But I guess that was a situation where it might have been better to have had a little less to drink.

WE WERE NOT TRAPPED, PART III

THE THING ABOUT BRIBING a border guard, or any official person, is that you've got to remember that you're not really bribing a border guard — you're bribing a *human being*. A human being with dreams, with dislikes, with a desire for some semblance of dignity, and if you're lucky, a human being with a sense of humour. And of course, it helps if they're a smoker.

Most of all, you've got to have confidence. Real confidence. And somehow, that morning when I woke up, I had it. Somehow, I knew, on that day, this was the day, maybe the one day of my whole life, that God had given me, when I could Do No Wrong. No cocaine was involved in my mood, either. I just had a true sense of Destiny, of the alignment of all the forces of chance and the unseen currents of the events that shape men's lives, roaring behind me like a set of nine diesel locomotives.

I don't know why, but nobody ever had to tell me how to finagle my way across the Yugoslav checkpoint on the border of Bosnia. Somehow, I just *knew*. Like I was born for it. It's strange, because eastern European corruption is so different from Canadian corruption.

A Canadian government minister doesn't need to take a bribe, say, from a company like Bombardier. Bob from Bombardier was in the same fraternity at university as the politicians, they all belong to the same country club. Bob gets the fat government contract, the government minister gets a seat on the board when he retires from politics, seven years later.

Sure, a small group of people who all know each other make out like bandits off the People's money, while the People get overpriced trains and concrete with too much sand and not enough cement, but it's not *corruption,* silly.

But in unstable places where you can't be sure that patience will bring the payoff, the exchanges are a lot more honest, a lot more clear, immediate. Honest — in that nobody is fooling *themselves* about what's actually going on.

Maybe that's why I've had so many troubles in Canada over the years. I don't connect well with the self-deluded, self-righteous Canadian style of corruption.

Anyway, the first thing I somehow just *knew* was that instead of driving the school bus and its load of black-clad chain-smoking Sarajevo alternative-culture intellectuals straight up to the checkpoint, it was better if we just parked over to the side, about thirty yards away.

"Everybody stay in the bus," I shouted. "Let me do the talking."

"Man, you don't even speak Serbian," pointed out Marko the Finnish metalhead.

"I can lie in any language. Now listen, after a while I might bring you out to talk to them. Just you, Marko. And make your Yugo-talk sound as Finnish-sounding as possible, you know? Make sure you've got an accent. Everybody else? Don't speak. Don't talk. Even if they talk to you, act like you don't understand. Just be cool and follow my lead. I know what I'm doing."

The English-speakers in the group translated for the others. For some reason, they just nodded their heads, stoically. Any of my friends back in Edmonton would have given me the finger and demanded to know what the fuck I thought I was up to. No man is a prophet in his own home, is what the Irish say.

I knew it was important, most of all, to appear as nonthreatening as possible. I needed to look anomalous, a Thing

Outside of the Known Narrative of the war. I needed to seem like an improbable freak. This is within the realm of my abilities.

That's why I skipped and hopped like a schoolgirl as I lugged the full-to-bursting checkered plaid plastic carry-all bags, singing "The Rodeo Song" at the top of my scratchy bullfrog voice.

> *Well, it's forty below and I don't give a fuck,*
> *Got a heater in the truck and it's off to the rodeo.*
> *Here comes Johnny with his pecker in his hand,*
> *He's a one-balled man and it's off to the rodeo.*

I often sing that song when I'm nervous, or drunk, or both. It takes me back to my childhood when my dad and my uncle would chunk it into the 8-track and sing along in the old red Dodge as we'd go rattling and bounding across the summer fields. Somehow it soothes me.

I could see the two border cops eyeing me as they leaned against the little guardhouse in their puke-and-shit-mix olive uniforms. They feigned disinterest, but I knew for a fact that I was the most entertaining thing they were gonna see all week. A crazy Canuck with bags full of goodies and a line of ridiculous bullshit.

"Hi there, fellas!" I waved and grinned like an idiot. They looked at each other. The younger one unbuttoned his pistol holster.

I waddled up to them, put one of the carryalls down and offered my right paw in a forceful, friendly manner to the one who hadn't unbuttoned his holster.

"Name's Cam Ouiniette, from Innisfail, Alberta, Canada. Pleased to meetcha!"

The guard didn't shake my hand, but I was unperturbed. The front pocket of my plaid shirt had a Bic lighter and a pack of the Canadian Consulate's Marlboros in it. I reached in with a dainty light touch, causing no stir or sense of threat in the guards, since the Marlboros were plainly visible poking up from the top. I pulled out a smoke, put it into my mouth, and offered a dart to the non-unbuttoned guard. After just a second's hesitation, he took it. Before I even lit it, I offered him the whole pack.

"Go on, take it, there's more where that came from."

The guy took the pack. The hook was set.

I set the carryall in between us and started ostentatiously rummaging in it. They stepped over to see what I was doing. I pulled up a bottle of Jack Daniels and held it in front of them. It shone like the golden, boozy promise of Freedom in the noonday early autumn sun. The green meadows of the valley caught the refracted light. The rocky hillsides smiled down on the bottle, instrument of Liberty.

"Care for a snort? I got some important stuff I need to discuss with you." I gestured over to the card table they had set up outside, next to the guard box. A pleasant place to pass the time.

I can be a surprisingly patient man when I'm comfortably seated, drinking hard liquor. The number three is a magic number. I waited for us to look each other in the eyes and down the third shot before I began to broach the subject at hand.

"My friends, it's essential that I get these Canadian Rock Stars to Italy."

The men shook their head. Was it a "no" head shake? No. It was an "I don't know what the fuck you're saying, Creature from Outer Space" head shake.

"Marko! Get over here, willya? Marko!"

Marko jogged up the grassy hill, his dreads bouncing. He was pale, shaky. Like a rookie hopeful trying to show some hustle at the team tryouts.

"Okay. You tell them: I am the Tour Manager. This is a Big Rock Band from Canada. "Machine Vivisection Anatomy Laboratory" is the name of the band. Industrial Noise Music. Very popular in Germany. Very popular."

Marko translated. The guards looked over at the bus, impassively.

"We were going to Vienna, to play, and our son-of-a-whore driver got drunk in the night. Took a wrong turn into Bosnia."

Translation. Muted chuckling.

"Okay, bad luck. We fired that motherfucker, you bet your ass. Then, the hotel we stayed at — in the middle of the night — the entire staff ran away!" I gesticulated wildly, a man driven half-crazy by misfortune. "Can you believe that? Ask them if they can believe that. Unbelievable bullshit. Ask them!"

Marko asked them. They shook their heads. Was it a "Yeah, it defies belief how many people don't have any pride in their work, their duties," sympathetic head shake, or was it a "No, I genuinely don't believe you." head shake? I think at that point it was a deliberately ambiguous head shake. They hadn't made up their minds what they were going to do.

"And worse than that, they stole our passports that we left at the desk for safekeeping! I tell you, we don't have this kind of thing happen in Canada. No sir. Sons of bitches!"

As Marko spoke, the older guard nodded, with a half-smile. He knew where this was headed.

"So. I have a letter here from the Canadian Consulate, explaining the situation." I waved the meaningless, semi-purloined document with its distinctive maple leaf letterhead. "The procedure is, you're supposed to hold on to this for your files. This'll cover your ass if anybody asks any annoying questions. Another drink?"

I handed over the paper as I filled the glasses. We knocked another one back.

"Oh, there's another important issue: We won't be able to take all this liquor and tobacco we've got here across the Italian border, because we don't have enough cash with us to pay the customs duties, which are outrageous. The Italians are all thieves, as I'm sure you know. So we're gonna have to leave them here. Can we leave it with you guys for safekeeping?"

Marko imparted this to the pair. The younger one said something that made the older one laugh, slap his thighs, jump up suddenly, and shout "Hoy!"

I turned to Marko. "What, they just celebrating their haul? What'd he say?"

"He says that before you can go, since you are Big Rock Stars, you should give a little concert for them, so they can hear your music."

"Ha, ha ha!"

The guard laughed.

I laughed.

Everybody laughed.

Then the guard said something.

"He says 'No, really.' They want a concert."

I had little time to prep the gloomy bus inmates.

"OKAY, JUST DON'T SAY *anything*. Just chant, like, 'Ahh, ah, ah ah!' And just bang the shit out of the bus with whatever comes to hand. Make it *rhythmic* somehow. Put every aspect of your anxiety about this moment into your performance. It's got to be convincing."

And it was.

I would go so far as to say that my Bosnian Crowley-ites didn't *pretend* to be the Industrial-Noise-Rock band Machine Vivisection Anatomy Laboratory — they *formed* this band, for one performance only. Wailing their angst and whaling away on that school bus with tire irons, wrenches, some of the harder luggage, a metal thermos or two — whatever came to hand. The blond quiet guy just banged away at the rear left fender with his bare fists till they were bloody.

"So, what do you think? Eh?" I myself was pretty impressed with the power and density of the sound these people were creating. It was a fantastic musical moment. I wish I had a vinyl pressing of that moment in my hands right now.

The older guard took a luxurious drag on his Marlboro and said something, deadpan. The younger one laughed.

"What's that, Marko? What'd he say?"

"He says that with umm, a 'bad noise' like that, *they* should be bribing *you* to leave the country."

I was genuinely offended, I tell you. Some people just have no taste.

As the bus laboured away, I took a long pull on one of the bottles that remained. We hadn't even had to give them all away. Someone turned on a ghetto blaster. It was Supertramp. "Bloody Well Right," a band and a song I'd always despised for its slickness, softness, and pretentions to classical music influences. But right then, I suddenly felt a surge of warmth for the thrust of the melody, the repetition of the word *right*. Then Marko slammed his fist on the Eject button and popped in Keskonen Suoli's first album, and I felt even better as the guitar riff introduced itself briefly before the brutal bass and drums thundered in like a glorious, galloping herd of muskox the size of mountains.

Marko leapt up and began thrashing up and down the aisles, banging his head in ecstasy.

A small, cold hand took mine. I turned to look in the beautiful, sad eyes of Marina, Marko's girlfriend.

"I have not been in love with Marko for some time," she intoned, dolefully shaking her head.

"Oh, that's too bad," I said. It did not dampen my elation. I tried to look empathetic.

Sadly, she shook her head again. She sighed, partly in exasperation.

"No, you don't understand."

"No, I'm really sorry."

"I think I may be falling in love with *you*," she said, with a shrug of hopeless disbelief.

That moment when you said that, my Love, was the greatest moment, of the greatest day of my life.

ATTACKED

ONCE I WAS FINISHED illuminating the Widow Rogers about the errors of her ways, I grabbed my Caesar (I think it was mine) and headed out of the coffee shop. I believe that some of the bruises I later found on my legs and face were from the fall I took between tables when some inconsiderate gimp left their crutches poking out from under their chair, and the now-frayed bathrobe caught on them. You bet I gave him a piece of my mind.

I could feel myself crashing hard, so I was desperately searching for an appropriate place to lie down. But nowhere seemed quite appropriate enough. I remember myself stumbling onward, onward, toward the festival grounds, but I don't have a clear memory of actually vaulting the fence, somehow, or the decision to lie down in the long grass under the outdoor tent stage where Mykola was due to perform at another workshop five hours later. So you have to credit me, that even in my lowest, most anaesthetized state, I still had an intuitive sense of where I ought to be.

All I know is, I woke up and I was under attack.

From the blackness of my inebriated sleep, I felt a hand slap my face. I'm a man who reacts quickly to danger, so when the hand slapped me again, and then a third time, I sprang into action, even before I'd taken full stock of the situation, or the size, or identity of my assailant. There was no time to wonder, *Which of the people*

who've threatened revenge upon me at one time or another could it be?
It was anyone's guess.

I swore valiantly and grabbed hold of his arm. But he was even quicker than me, because he somehow instantly grabbed hold and wrestled me into a prone position on the grass, pushing the heel of his palm into my face — clearly someone with martial-arts training. Now my eyes were forced shut, further delaying any attempt to discover my enemy.

We thrashed around in the dark under that stage, me, shouting and cursing, he, silent as a ninja assassin, following my every attempt to break free with an equal and brutal counter-move. Somehow, I had to dislodge him. I've been trained by long experience brawling on the beer-soaked floors of Alberta taverns, and also on the beer-soaked floor of the kitchen that I grew up in, where my father would administer his soused version of discipline. I learned early that there's no such thing as fighting dirty, just fighting for survival, for escape. So I had no compunction about grabbing hold of the bastard's hand, leaning up and taking a huge, tearing, vicious bite. I felt the flesh rip and thought I heard a crunch of bone. Blood flowed into my mouth. But I heard no scream, although he did counterattack immediately.

An inkling of pain flowed into my mind from somewhere. The dull, soggy processors in my cerebellum slowly sorted out the source of it — the villain had hit me precisely tit-for-tat, stabbing me in my right hand.

With a mighty heave, I rolled over and out from under the stage, with the idea of exposing this psycho to the public. With more room to move, I started flailing about, trying to shake him. "Holy shit!" somebody shouted, and I opened my eyes. I looked around. Where was the sonofabitch?

Various people nearby were staring at me, edging away with looks of shock and disgust. A guy in a tie-dyed shirt and sandals, some kids with a Frisbee. A couple of old ladies. None of them could have scrambled away quick enough to have been the culprit.

The cruel truth of the matter crept up on me slowly. I re-traced my memory of the last few minutes, looking for an alternative scenario, as I sat there, bleeding. But there was no getting around the fact that I had just bitten my own right hand to hell. I guess I'd been sleeping at a funny angle, and my entire right arm had lost circulation, pressed under my own weight. I blinked at the realization, tasting my own blood, watching it flow all over my bathrobe and spatter my track pants. I screamed. The people moved farther away.

It was hot, and I was hemorrhaging profusely. I slowly crawled myself up to a sitting position, tore a strip out of the terry cloth, and fashioned a makeshift tourniquet to wrap around the spurting wound. I reflected that one good thing about biting yourself is that you don't have to get tested for rabies or hepatitis or anything, since you already know the medical history of the person who bit you. At least I wouldn't need any shots.

HIDE THE GRAIN

OF COURSE I HADN'T ACTUALLY consciously chosen to lie down under Stage Five in order to be present for the "Veterans and Rookies" workshop. That was instinctive decision-making, for which, as you know by now, I have quite a knack. It took me a minute or two to adjust my eyes and figure out where I was.

Leslie had put Mykola and some other younger folkies up against some of the old fossils from the early days of Canadian folk. These were people who started out back when you could make a reasonably good career and probably sell over twenty thousand LPs with some fake bluegrass and a few hippie ballads about the calming, sweet beauty of life on Vancouver Island. Sheesh.

The old folksinger got up to his feet and said, "Well, I'm going to play a song that may surprise you. Last February, I was asked to contribute some music to a documentary for CTV called *Point of Blue*. Now this doc follows the Vancouver Police as they do their thankless job in the Downtown Eastside. Some of these people in the Downtown Eastside have fallen through the cracks of the system, some might say they've jumped *into* the cracks, but that's another matter. The point is that a lot of these fellas *(and gals)* who work down there are really going the extra mile to try to help the people down there to get out of the cycle of addiction."

Now I know that people are *supposed* to drift to the right as they age, but I tell you, he then proceeded to play an almost unbelievably reactionary song, a *paean* to the goodness and caring of the Vancouver Police Department. I personally on several occasions have seen members of this fine force laughing as they pepper-sprayed junkies just for the sheer fun of watching them squirm and writhe. Pretty awful stuff, this. But on a sunny Sunday afternoon, with the guitar finger-picking in a pleasant, rolling way, and the folksinger's low, mellow voice lulling along, it all just kind of washed over the crowd like a warm, not-very-cryptic fascism bath. The song finished, and there was the *de rigueur* applause.

Mykola picked up his instrument. He stood up. He took a deep breath.

"I'd like to dedicate this song to Frank Paul, who died of hypothermia this past winter, when he was dragged, unconscious from the drunk tank at the Vancouver Municipal pre-trial centre in the Downtown Eastside, and left lying in the rain in an alley between Hastings and Cordova Street. Nobody on duty at the time will admit to seeing this happen. And no one in the Vancouver Police Department is willing to say which of their members is responsible. I've translated the song from the original Ukrainian. It's a song from the Ukrainian famine of the 1930s, where over two million people died. It's called 'Hide the Grain.' The chorus translates as 'Hide the Grain, hide the grain, mother, but hide it well, for if they find the grain the police will shoot us. The police serve power, they do not serve justice, hide the grain.'"

I can't play it for you now. I can't use words to describe the *way* he played it. Nothing I could write would suffice.

But as much as you, reader, may want to pooh-pooh this notion, I am willing to swear, and *do* hereby swear on my daughter's life, that Mykola's song travelled outward in waves, changing lives as it went.

I saw a teenage boy standing with his conservative-looking parents. The parents were frowning, looking away from the stage, deliberately. But the boy stared, transfixed, exhilarated by what this chubby, goofy fellow with the odd instrument was doing on the stage.

I saw a very old woman. Who knows? She may not have lost family in that famine, a lifetime ago. Maybe she wasn't even Ukrainian. But nevertheless, the tears were streaming, flooding the dry riverbeds of the wrinkles on her face as she shook. Another old lady next to her turned and took her arm and leaned her head on her shoulder, and they both wept together.

And then I spotted Sandy Mackenzie at the edge of the crowd, just listening, eyes closed, like he used to do when we brought those strange records back from the shop and played them in his mother's basement, before everything went to shit between us.

He opened his eyes and he looked up, and caught sight of me looking at him, as Mykola's song tore through the air. He looked at me, and he made a little head gesture towards Mykola. Then he gave a rueful little smile, and the slightest little nod. And I knew exactly what he meant.

Mykola came to the finishing home chord, and let it ring. All around, the crowd was silent, gaping at the power of the seventy-year-old song.

I REALIZED THAT MY WORK HERE was essentially done. I had achieved the transcendent moment of the festival. And I was seized with a violent urge to get the Hell out of there before anything fucked up this feeling. I figured Mykola and them would understand. They were true artists, after all. Sure, they might be a little pissed off about not getting paid and having no immediately evident way to get home to Vancouver, 1,200 kilometres away, but I knew that they'd get quite a bit of money from sales at the merchandise tent, and they could always bum a ride home with somebody who wanted to sleep with them or something. Musicians always get by on their charm, anyway.

I LIMPED MY WAY TO THE GATES of the festival, taking care not to make eye contact with anybody, so that I wouldn't get drawn into any conversations that might wreck my mood. Nobody seemed to want to come within twenty feet of me — I guess I just gave off that "don't talk to me" vibe, and then also of course there was the facial bruises, the all-over filth and dead prairie grass, the torn, blood-soaked bathrobe, and the open, suppurating wound that I'd made of my right hand.

I walked out the main gate, and lo and behold, there were the Supersonic Grifters. They weren't playing. Just standing around, passing a smoke between them. They also looked a bit off. Maybe not as off as me, but off.

"What's the matter, kids?"

"Security called the cops on us last night in the hotel lobby. Jacob started lipping them off so they hauled him to the drunk tank. So we just spent our last money bailing him out."

"Yeah, and you did all the coke while I was in the can. Why does this always happen to *me*?" Jacob kicked the fence with a worn combat boot. "I just wanna fucken *break something!*"

"Hunh, that was a lot of coke to do in one night."

"We called it the Blizzard of '03."

The feral little fiddler was still chipper. She held up her right hand, which was shaking visibly. "My bow hand's got n-n-natural vibra-a-a-to. I don't even have to doo-oo-oo anything."

I had a sudden impulse. I took the laminated, all-access pass from around my neck, and put it around the fiddler's.

"Well here ya go. It's my gift to you."

I knew I didn't have to explain to these little criminals about getting themselves all in, one at a time, through different gates by passing the pass back out through a hole in the fence. In twenty minutes they'd all be loose in the festival, and the Devil would ride. I walked on, leaving them to their celebration dance, imagining all the transformative experiences that were now pre-ordained for the unsuspecting festival-goers.

I found the minivan, gunned the engine, and tore out of the parking lot of the Westin. And I haven't looked back, I tell you. That's how I operate.

THE GAMBLING
NORWEGIAN FARMER

A GUY IN STAVANGER, NORWAY, once told me this story:

He said his great-grandfather was a farmer in a little town, about 100 kilometres outside Oslo, back in about 1905, when 100 kilometres out of town was really the sticks. He owned a decent-sized farm that had been in the family for generations. He had a wife and twelve kids. He had a reputation for being tight-fisted when it came to spending money on his family.

This great-grandfather got into a poker game on a Saturday night. At this poker game was a bunch of other farmers from the area, plus a Stranger, an Outsider, a travelling professional gambler.

The farmer started to lose, and lose big, to this professional gambler. When normally sober, hard-working people hit a run of bad luck, they can fall into a trap that tells them that they just have to try even harder and their good fortune will return. The Lord rewards hard work, and all that. This is not a good strategy at poker. Soon the farmer had lost all the cash he possessed.

The guy who told me this story didn't offer any insight into the farmer's interior life. He just told me what he did. What he did was, he bet everything — and I mean *everything* — on his next hand.

And of course he lost. He got up from the table and left.

* * *

THE GUY WHO TOLD ME THIS STORY, he says he heard it from his grandfather, the youngest of the twelve children of that farmer who lost the poker game. The grandfather would have been around six or seven at the time of the story.

According to the Norwegian guy who told me the story, his grandfather says that the morning after the poker game, Sunday morning, a stranger rode up to the farmhouse.

This stranger walked into the kitchen, took off his hat, and sat down.

He calmly informed the wife and twelve children that he had won them and the farm in a poker game, and that their father and husband would not be returning.

He went outside and hitched the good white horses to the family wagon. The storyteller said that his grandfather emphasized the fact that the stranger chose the fancy white horses, which the original farmer had never used for the family wagon, because the farmer had always firmly maintained that the fancy horses were "too good to waste" on such things.

The stranger told the wife and twelve children to get in the wagon. They obeyed, and the gambler drove his new family into town for Sunday church services.

The stranger stayed with his new family, and before long, according to the boy who grew up to be the storyteller's grandfather, everyone, *everyone* agreed that the stranger was a better father, farmer, and husband than the original. He lived there happily, to the end of his long life.

The original great-grandfather was never seen again. And no one thought to look for him.

TIRED

GOD, I'M SO AWFULLY TIRED. My body's tired. Brain won't go to sleep. Need to move.

BACK

I JUST WENT FOR A WALK out into the fields and have now returned. And I have received a sign. Here's how it happened:

Big summer moon out, lighting the neglected, bruised prairie like a film set, day for night. I leapt from the remnants of the front porch like a swimmer jumping off the dock into a vast, golden, fucked-up ocean.

The light breeze touched me, making me feel physically connected to the whole endless sky. I wasn't tired anymore. I moved without feeling my legs. Headed down the short driveway, turned left onto the dirt road, unfenced dried-out canola and scrub on either side of me glowing in the moonlight.

Alberta prairie is flat in the general sense, but there's contours to it. Little rolling depressions and low bunkers that make shadows and hide things. I trekked on, my arms out for balance, embracing the stars.

I don't worry about bats. Bats eat bugs, which get up people's noses sometimes. When I saw one or two of their black flickering shapes in the sky, I felt no disquiet.

AND WHEN I HEARD THE COYOTE, rather than disquiet, I felt kinship of course. Who doesn't love Coyote, the survivor with the rueful grin? Only evil bastards who want the world to be boring.

I thought I saw him move through some scrub, far, far off to the right, out of the corner of my eye. I walked on.

The sky seemed to be breathing at me, heavily, as I pushed farther into the field. I heard howling again, but closer. I could feel the warm blood pumping in my body, specifically in my hands, down in the fingertips.

I saw movement again.

I pressed on, but I have to admit that the great beautiful dome of the sky was starting to recede in my mind, as I began to suspect that the coyote might in fact be following me.

At first I welcomed it. Let Brother Trickster Coyote approach. I had nothing to fear. Wasn't it right that we should commune on this strange, perfect night? Besides, they're actually quite small animals, and I'm a pretty big man, if I do say so myself.

But then I caught a dark snicker of movement in the tall grass to the *right* of me. And a few moments later, to the *left* again. And then was there something just ahead? You know how they move — they bounce, they lope. They don't run or walk like a mere man-dependant dog.

It suddenly occurred to me that there was more than one of them. People think of the coyote as a loner, and to be sure, his ability to work solo is what's enabled him to adapt and triumph in places where the wolf, who needs the sociability of a pack, finds only futility.

But that doesn't mean that coyotes *don't ever* work together in packs, like they used to before they became stalkers of garbage and suburban neighbourhood cats.

And when they worked in packs, they could take down a buffalo, you know.

I was very aware of this.

I turned and faced the house. It was smaller than I'd remembered it, and there was a big cloud of dust in the field of view. I must have been travelling faster and more vigorously than I'd realized.

As I walked back, it was like I'd entered into a different world than the one I'd walked out into. It was a split-in-half world, part of which held a future where I ran back into the farmhouse and bolted the door, and in the other future, I offered myself up as prey, to be torn apart into oblivion. They say that at the moment of ultimate defeat, the hunted animal feels no pain. It goes into a trance after it drops to its knees, exhausted, and gives up the chase to the hunter.

I didn't run, but I marched with purpose. It only crept up on my consciousness gradually that in fact I did want to escape.

I kept seeing flicks of dark movement here and there, pursuing me, subtly, trickily, inevitably.

OKAY, NOW I KNOW THIS next part you're just not going to believe. Not only because at this point in my "career" I guess everybody thinks I lie about everything. Also because the obvious implications are so clear. And of course I didn't have anybody else with me, or a camera, so you're just going to have to take my word on it, which you probably won't, but this definitely happened — I did not make it up, nor was it some kind of speed-jag comedown hallucination:

A white horse. A real, breathing, dusty-legged horse cantered toward me out of the field to my left. A mare. Not entirely white; there was some grey dappling on her flanks and her neck. The unkempt mane was a darker grey, but that could have been the dust again. She was skinny, like maybe she hadn't been eating so well, but her legs looked strong. No saddle, no halter.

I know you won't believe this part, either, but she came right up to me. She slowed as she approached, till she was just tentatively walking by the time she was, say, fifteen yards away.

I thought unthreatening thoughts and relaxed my body, and she continued her approach. I reached out to her gently, and she sniffed my hand. I stroked her nose, then her face, then her neck.

The horse looked around, and I looked around. The farmhouse wasn't so small now, and there was no sign of the coyotes as we walked up the road.

We were about ten yards from the driveway when the horse just seemed to decide it was time to go. She turned and started walking off. I thought of trying to bring her back to the farmhouse, maybe get her to jump up onto the porch, where I could protect her, but I had no halter anywhere about and besides, since she seemed to have magically dispelled the coyote pack, I figured she would be okay out there.

After I climbed up the porch steps I turned to look for her, but she had disappeared into the landscape.

GONE

IT'S TIME TO GO. My purpose holds.

POSTSCRIPT
by Geoff Berner

ON MY RETURN JOURNEY FROM my research trip in the Maramureş region of Romania last August, I was struck for a second time by a parasite borne of well-water that I had glugged gratefully in a small village near Cluj-Napoca. I know that drinking village well-water isn't advisable, but I had found myself severely dehydrated by my efforts to be culturally sensitive and match the drinking habits of my Roma hosts.

I was taken off the airplane at Pearson International Airport in Toronto and spent the next few weeks at St. Joseph's Hospital, in a stewy fog of pain and terror that dissipated only slowly.

So I was longer coming home to Vancouver than I had planned, and longer getting out and about. Which is to explain why it was mid autumn before I found out about the disappearance, after the Calgary Folk Festival, of my old friend and manager Campbell Ouiniette.

As soon as I could muster the necessary strength, I set out for the prairies in search of him. Not to disparage the work of the Royal Canadian Mounted Police, but it was relatively easy for me to find Campbell's route and catch up with the elderly farmer who sold him his farmhouse. The rental-car companies put a satellite tracker in their vehicles nowadays. Maybe Cam was aware of this, because the document which you have just read was sitting on the kitchen table, held down by a rock. It was a much simpler task to find the document than to decipher it, given the furious nature of the man's handwriting.

Unfortunately, that's where the trail ends. No one seems to have seen him, and he seems to have gotten in touch with no one. No one who's talking, at any rate.

As much as I hate to entertain the thought, I don't rule out the possibility that he has drowned, by accident or by design, in one of the many fierce rivers of the Canadian prairie. He always had a penchant for floating down the Bow, North Saskatchewan, and Fraser rivers, naked in an inner tube with a flat of Old Style Pilsner beer bobbing beside him. And this may sound irrational, but when I last saw him, in June, his skin had an odd translucence that reminded me of the last time I saw our mutual friend Morten, who died in the river that runs past Fredrikstad. By accident or design. Bodies that drown in fierce rivers are often never found, and ones that are found are so badly altered that they require DNA tests to identify them.

The government of Alberta has been on a service-cutting spree lately, so that may be the reason why there has been no great effort made by the Mounties to find Cam, and no effort by the various coroners' offices to test Cam's hair sample against the catalogue of unidentified human remains discovered in Alberta and Saskatchewan that summer.

Or it may have something to do with the fact that when I filled out the "identifying marks" part of Cam's missing persons form, I listed, along with the pentagrams, the tattoo on his left shoulder that reads "Fuck The Police!" In retrospect, I admit that may have been an error on my part.

At any rate, my efforts to have this book published were made in the hopes that some of the proceeds from sales may go to fund lab tests that could possibly solve the mystery for us, and bring closure for Campbell's family, who miss him very much. There's also the possibility that if Cam *is* alive, and he sees his name in print somewhere, wherever he is, he'll come out of the woodwork to try to collect his royalties.

Many people who were involved with, or know of the events described in the above document may wish to point out the various flaws, inconsistencies, impossibilities, outright fabrications, and unforgivable slanderous lies that appear in the narrative. When I first began typing out the manuscript, it was my sincere intention to mark the text as I went along, in order to include a section of footnotes at the back, correcting each transgression against accuracy and decency. But unfortunately that job soon became so overwhelming that my immune system broke down completely, and I experienced a second relapse of my parasite, which it seems will be with me always.

This Book As It Is Now Could Never Have Existed Without the Invaluable Help of:

Wayne Adams, Ralph Allen, Margot Berner, Nancy Berner, Sarge Berner, Shaughnessy Bishop-Stall, Dennis E. Bolen, Benny Bratten, Genevieve Buechner, Kerry Clarke, Marek Colek, Jim Cuddy, Diona Davies, Susan de Cartier, Kris Demeanor, Tanya Gillis, Randy Iwata, Heather John, Corb Lund, Carolyn Mark, Justin Newall, C. Noyes, Stuart Parker, Pat Shewchuck, Jeremy Stewart, Angela Teistler, Shannon Whibbs, Shena Yoshida, Karina Zeidler, Maryse Zeidler, Paulette Zeidler, Joseph Zeidler-Berner.

Thank you for being indispensable.

A Note to Music Lovers:

As a special bonus, this novel comes with a downloadable high-quality digital album of great artists covering Geoff Berner's songs. To access this album, go to *www.geoffberner.com* and type in the following password: gsgb91mzib97jphzb03unzb13

Track listing for *Festival Man*, the album:

1. Whiskey Rabbi — Kaizers Orchestra
2. Liar's Bridge – ESL
3. That's What Keeps the Rent Down — Corb Lund and the Hurtin' Albertans
4. Prairie Wind — Carolyn Mark and Her New Best Friends
5. Victory Party Variations — Orchid Ensemble
6. This Authentic Klezmer Wedding Band Is For Hire — Rot Front
7. Phoney Drawl — Dave Lang
8. The Rich Will Move to the High Ground — Kris Demeanor and Cutest Kitten Ever!
9. Unlistenable Song — Rae Spoon
10. Light Enough to Travel — Real Ones
11. Volcano God — Wax Mannequin
12. Wealthy Poet — Maria in the Shower
13. Public Relations — The Burnettes
14. Iron Grey — Mr Johnson's Grade 5/6 Kittens from École Macphail Memorial in Flesherton, Ontario, directed by Charlie Glasspool
15. Cherry Blossoms — Kim Barlow and Blue Hibou

Visit us at
Dundurn.com
@dundurnpress
Facebook.com/dundurnpress
Pinterest.com/dundurnpress